TWISTED SECRETS

DEADLY ISLES SPECIAL OPS, BOOK 1

AMY MCKINLEY

ARROWSCOPE PRESS, LLC

Twisted Secrets

Copyright © 2020 Amy McKinley

(p) **ISBN-13**: 978-1-951919-02-3

(e) **ISBN-13**: 978-1-951919-01-6

Publisher: Arrowscope Press, LLC; www.arrowscopepress.com

Editing— Kate B., Line Editor, Taylor A., Proofreader, Red Adept Editing

Cover Design—T.E. Black Designs; www.teblackdesigns.com

Author photo provided by—Brookelyn Anhalt of lovely.life.photography; https://www.facebook.com/LovelyLifePhotography-102253596490708

Interior Formatting & Design— Arrowscope Press, LLC; www.arrowscopepress.com

XANDER

The *whomp-whomp-whomp* sound of the blades filled the interior of the helicopter. My unease rode passenger in the empty seat next to me, mocking me with the reminder of the failed mission. The one that had cost us our commander's life and injured our brother—my actual brother.

Next time would be different. No other outcome was acceptable.

The night sky was dark, as the crescent moon shed little light. Below us, thick trees formed a canopy above the ground. Adrenaline pumped through me, and I tensed as we closed in on the drop point west of the Colombian-Venezuelan border. In the back of my mind, a familiar hollowness reappeared. My brother's injury and honorable discharge weighed heavily. But that wasn't the only thing that bothered me. For a long time, all I'd needed was the adventure, firepower, and missions, until lately. *Something's missing.* Dammed if I knew what it was.

The helo descended, and I emptied my mind of all thoughts unrelated to the mission. We would fast-rope from thirty feet then take what the enemy meant to use against us. Under cover of the inky sky, the Black Hawk descended deep into the

Colombian mountain range's dense jungle, which bordered Cúcuta near the war-torn Venezuelan border. Not far from where we converged on the ground below, our informant would meet us. From there, we would close in on a building rumored to house a stockpile of weapons potentially meant for use against the United States.

A sea of trees was below. I waited. A small clearing came into view, barely visible with the minimal light from the moon.

We were ghosts going into the darkness. If caught, our country would deny our existence. We knew the risks.

Our lines dangled above the ground, as we weren't jumping with parachutes but fast-roping. With night vision goggles and backpack in place, I pulled thick gloves on then looped the rope around my non-dominant leg—the other foot would clamp over the top to assist with breaking. At the pilot's order, all six of us dropped from the helo with ropes secured between our gloved hands and feet. The helicopter blades whirled above, and the wind rushed past. In a matter of seconds, I squeezed my hands, which slowed my drop dramatically. The ground approached quickly, and when I touched down, I bent my knees to absorb the impact.

Through thick, leafy branches, all six of us slid to the ground below. We released the ropes soundlessly. The whirl of the helo as it banked away was the only foreign sound. My team gathered beneath a large tree before heading east to the coordinates we'd received from the informant, confirmed by both satellite infrared imaging and our handheld GPS devices.

All that existed was the mission and our role in securing the weapons. We'd gone over our approach, and each of us knew our position, the expectations for intervening with the informant, and what to do afterwards.

The jungle was displayed in a thermal layering of greens through our night goggles. With our weapons locked and loaded, we looked to Daryl, our relatively new team leader, for the order to move out. He gave the hand signal, and we shifted into a single-file formation, guns up and ready. He led us through the thick jungle teeming with hostiles. Our guards up, we moved swiftly but with care to make as little noise as possible. A mile out, we came upon the clearing where the informant waited. A vehicle would then take us to the target building and the cache of weapons inside.

We were at the tail end of the dry season, early April. It was hot as hell, and the scent of rotting vegetation surrounded us. The mesh netting in our combat clothing protected us from the mosquitos and other insects. It wasn't long until we reached the coordinates on the edge of the jungle that flanked the metropolitan area. No one stepped from the shadows to greet us.

My gut tightened from the bad omen that had stalked us on our flight. *Something's not right...* As with our last fubar mission, I felt it deep in my bones.

We absorbed the rhythm of the jungle, taking its measure as we crept forward. The informant was a no-show, but we were mere steps from the building where we were to meet. A hush descended the closer we crept, the usual night sounds absent.

Daryl gave the signal to stop. We'd rehearsed him leading us in. Kyle would go next, and I was behind him with the rest of our unit holding up the rear. With a hand signal from our team leader, Daryl, Kyle moved up in front. Another jolt of unease punched me in the gut. *Why?* I clenched my teeth, the last-minute change from a well-rehearsed and planned mission grating on my already taut nerves.

Kyle shoved the door open as I peered around Daryl. *Goddammit.* Kyle and Daryl shouted to retreat. I whirled around with the rest and sprinted to the edge of the forest. We hustled, but the blast caught us not far from the doorway.

On the floor of that barren room had been the informant, a bullet through the head, his body rigged with C-4 explosives.

Shit! It's a setup.

The blast took me to the ground. *Move! Move!* I yelled at myself. A piercing drone rung in my ears, and the ground spun as I tried to right myself. Dragging my hands close to my chest, I pushed up on one knee. Something hit my shoulder, hard. It took me back down, and I landed in the dirt again, pain flaring down the right side of my body. But adrenaline kept most of it at bay.

I sensed the thud of a body, forced myself to my feet again, and whipped around. Immediately, I locked on the body that lay a couple feet away from me. *Kyle.* Liquid oozed from the back of his neck. In less than a second, I was crouched by his prone body.

Daryl stood over us, alert and sweeping for hostiles. I didn't expect that to be it.

Tearing at the Velcro on my right side, I pulled out the hemostatic agent and poured the granules over his neck and open head gash. That would stop the bleeding until we could reassess. I hoped the oozing substance was only blood and not spinal fluid.

A handful of the granules went to my injury, pressing it into the torn flesh before I hoisted Kyle over my shoulder. Gunfire cut through the open area just as we took off. Daryl covered us as we tore through thick brush, branches slapping our faces and arms, bullets peppering the air around us. There'd been a slight delay in the gunfire—maybe the hostiles responded to the explosion, but chances were better that they were part of the trap.

We tunneled into the brush and wove through the trees, but dread stalked us, as it wasn't the first ambush.

———

TWO WEEKS LATER

THE DULL ACHE in my shoulder barely registered as I crossed Pearl Harbor's base then pushed through the building's entrance to find Daryl, our new team leader. Anger pulsed aggressively through me, as did the conversation I'd had yesterday with my girlfriend—ex-girlfriend, Carly.

Unwelcome, yesterday's encounter replayed through my mind. I'd been in the rehab room, one day away from being released, working on the exercises to strengthen my shoulder.

I couldn't stop the smile when Carly had crept into the room. Her curly shoulder-length dirty-blond hair fell around her heart-shaped face. Everything about her was soft and inviting. It'd been too long since I'd seen her, which I realized was unusual. Even so, I welcomed her beautiful face until I got a better look at her expression. Tears fell from her eyes, and her voice sounded devoid of strength. I stiffened, waiting for the blow.

"I wanted to wait to tell you when you were home, but"—she tugged at the hem of her fitted white T-shirt, her gaze skirting to the big windows rather than remaining on me—"I was already here. I-I met someone else."

I ground my teeth, waiting for her to continue, wondering if she would tell me who or why she couldn't wait for me to come home. I thought we'd had something good. We'd never fought, and she'd seemed happy. Things had been good between us, or so I thought. A cold numbness stole over my body, and I schooled my features so as not to reveal emotion. "Who?"

She inched back, her hand fumbling for the door. "We met at the beach, and we just clicked." Her voice was barely a whisper. "I'm sorry. It's Daryl." She turned and fled.

Rage flooded me. *Goddammit!* I turned and slammed my fist into the closest wall. Blood welled around my knuckles, the pain slow to register. I didn't know who I was angrier at, Carly or Daryl. That told me more than I wanted to know.

With the new day, I'd shoved my feelings about Carly down

deep. But Daryl—that poaching motherfucker. *He's to blame for more than taking her.* After this, I wanted to find fault in everything Daryl did. A cold son of a bitch, he'd changed our mission at the last second and for no apparent reason—switching the order of entry from himself to Kyle. Not only that, but Kyle hadn't survived. The head and neck wounds where large shrapnel had caught him had leaked with both blood and spinal fluid.

How the hell am I supposed to trust Daryl? After John had died, Daryl was assigned to our unit through temporary addition orders. He was my brother Ty's unit leader, something Ty and I would discuss very soon.

Daryl and I needed to talk.

When our team returned from that last mission, there had been other pressing concerns, including dealing with the death of one of our own as well as several injured. In a matter of minutes, I would walk from the hospital. The release papers were in my pocket. I'd stayed to complete the last few required PT exercises, but that was done.

I shoved out of the rehab center's double doors, stalked down the hallway, and pushed out of the exit door into the bright sunlight. Unable to deal with or change Carly's decision, I would focus on Daryl and what had gone down in Colombia.

I was finally out of the hospital, and I wanted answers.

The most pressing question surrounded that last mission, where we'd been ambushed. One casualty was bad, but it could have been worse. I'd escaped with shrapnel imbedded in my shoulder. Those were the risks we took, even though I still had a bad feeling about what had gone down.

The shrapnel had been surgically removed days before, and enough time had gone by that the Navy cleared me to leave the military hospital. I'd passed all the physical tests, and my injury, while tender, was healing nicely. It could have been worse. Being at the hospital for the amount of time they'd ordered wasn't what I wanted or felt was needed, but as the military looked at all SEALs as military property—valuable and expensive weapons—I hadn't had much choice.

That mission was stuck on repeat in my mind.

Without pause, I headed to the conference room where Daryl and my brother Ty were. Ty had been assigned to my SEAL unit through temporary addition order while I was away. Daryl bent over a laptop, and Ty stood nearby with his fists planted on the long table. He didn't look happy.

I entered the room, and Ty took one look at my face then rounded the table and shut the door, sealing the three of us in.

"Xander, I got the message that you'd been released and cleared for active duty. Good to have you back," Daryl said.

"Is it?" I growled. "Colombia was your first mission with us and second consecutive ambush. We barely made it out of the jungle, and I, for one, have some questions."

"Careful." Daryl swiveled in his chair until we were face-to-face, his glacial glare warning me to watch my step. "I realize you're upset about losing your teammate, but running your mouth will land you in a hell of a lot of trouble."

"It goes without saying that I'm upset. We all are." I tilted my head to the side and worked hard not to clench my fists as Ty resumed his former position at the table. "I have a question. After being stuck in the hospital, I had plenty of time to run through what happened that night, and something doesn't add up. Why did you change formation at the last minute?" *Had he known something we hadn't and put himself in a safer position? I wasn't ready to accuse him—I needed proof. But his instant reaction showed me that he got where I was going.*

A meaty fist slammed onto the table. Red infused Daryl's already ruddy face. "You're out of line." Daryl stood, his lips peeled back in a menacing growl. "Your doc and I are going to have a talk about your readiness to return to duty. Mentally, you're not there. Take the rest of the month off. The paperwork from him will soon follow."

Ty lurched around Daryl and cleared his throat. "Sorry, sir. It's just grief. Hard to come back the first time, and Kyle isn't here," he muttered, stepping between Daryl and me.

"I don't want to see your face until you've reevaluated the proper way to speak to your commander!" Daryl growled.

"Let's go, Xander," Ty said.

He whirled me around, and I let him. I didn't like Daryl, especially after Carly. I hadn't brought it up, but it had fueled my accusation—something I'm sure he'd known. Granted, things had gone too far on my end, and I was lucky that what I'd said had only resulted in forced leave. I hadn't meant to say what I had, but I hadn't been thinking rationally. On a personal level, there was no trust. And after Carly made her revelation, I'd had way too much time to think, and things weren't adding up.

"Christ, Xander." Ty's hand was wrapped tightly on the back of my neck as we plowed through the exit and into the bright sun. "There are questions, and then there're accusations. You're damn lucky you only got off with a slap on the wrist."

I clenched my teeth. "You know John would have never rolled over and accepted two back-to-back ambushes."

"There was an inquiry. You heard about the investigation and the lesson learned. Daryl isn't the cause."

"Do you know about Carly?"

Ty's features shuttered, and I could tell he understood the underlying source of my anger toward Daryl.

"Why the hell didn't you tell me?"

"I found out when I saw them together yesterday, and she begged me not to say anything to you. She was on her way to tell you." Ty squeezed my arm. "You weren't that into her, anyway."

"Doesn't matter," I growled.

"Yeah, I get it. Daryl fucked up and isn't the easiest to warm to. He does things differently in terms of communication. He's a bit standoffish, and I don't even know where to go with the stealing your girlfriend situation. That's not cool. I'm pissed for you. For now, try to keep that separate from the fact that he's leading your unit. He's good at what he does, and there must have been a reason for him to change the op at the last minute."

"It's all ego and secrets. If we can't trust him on a personal level, then he's not part of our team."

"I get it. You're pissed. I'm not happy about what he's done, either." Ty stopped, and we faced each other in the parking lot. "We'll figure this thing out. For now, you need to cool down. Go home, meet a girl you have a deeper connection with, and get lost in her for a while."

That's not something I had any hope for, as I'd never fallen for someone in the way he meant. I clapped my brother on the shoulder, checked my bad mood, then got in my truck. Once I was pointed in the direction of my condo in Honolulu, I thought about what he said. He wasn't wrong. I should have kept the discussion professional, wallowing in the loss of my girlfriend or in how much I wanted to kick Daryl's ass—which I still wanted to do. Instead, my thoughts returned to the failed op and what we must have missed. That last mission proved that something had to change.

2

RILEY

I stepped into the Coffee Hut and was surrounded by its familiar, rich aroma of roasted beans minutes before my shift started. The coffeehouse, where I worked with Chloe, Melanie, and our boss Jeffrey, was inviting with its dark wooden ceiling, brick interior walls, and soft lighting. After a few waves and exchanged greetings with our regulars, I slipped behind the bar then reached for my uniform, which I'd left on a hook in the small back room the day before. I tied a hasty bow, securing my black apron with the Coffee Hut's logo of a steaming coffee cup and the restaurant's name in loopy script beneath it.

"Hey, Riley." Ava's head popped up from her laptop, just noticing me, as she was engrossed in her work. "I didn't think you would make it in today."

"One of those mornings." I smiled at her as I rounded the counter and collected her empty cup. "Another?"

"You know it. Keep 'em coming." She looked over my shoulder and lowered her voice to a conspiratorial whisper. "Thank God you're here. Chloe makes them wrong."

Uncomfortable, I feigned a small laugh—my very likable

coworker tended to be a little heavy-handed on the creamer, and I knew Ava only liked a dash. "I've got you."

After greeting my coworkers, I got to work, only partially acknowledging the so-glad-you're-here echo and Chloe's narrowed glance at Ava. Ava had become a friend, but the blond woman was a handful. For some reason, she'd been nice to me, but to the others I knew of who rotated shifts with me, not so much.

As I made a new cup for Ava, I scanned the room furnished with four-tops and several oversized chairs with a table between them. All of our morning regulars were there. Ava was a writer and was in often, getting words in and guzzling coffee. She didn't normally do idle chitchat. Despite her work ethic and busy schedule, we'd somehow become friends.

A rustling sounded from the back room. Melanie exited minus her apron then sidled up next to me. "Hey, girl. Missed you at the Pizza Palace the other night. I thought you were going to hang with us?"

The grad department was small, and we tried to get together once in a while. Mel had picked the pizza restaurant, and I truly liked hanging out with her. She was one of my first friends at school, and we both crushed on our theory professor and advisor—but we stopped chatting about that after the first few weeks of school. Her sarcastic and sassy nature was infectious, and I wished I'd gone the other night.

"I was trying to catch up on homework and hadn't finished in time to go."

"You were missed." She tapped her nail on the counter and glanced at Ava, her face scrunched in distaste. "I don't know why you like her. She's a snob."

"Mel, Ava Murphy is a successful author, and you're a grad student in English." Based on that, Ava should have been an asset to her. We shared photography classes, but she was doing dual master's degrees. I honestly didn't pretend to understand writers.

She flipped her tawny hair over her shoulder and pushed away from the counter. Her shift was over, and it was clear she was ready to leave. "She's a *nonfiction* author. The only time I like to talk with her is about what we're reading—which are fiction books." Distaste dripped from her voice. "Besides, I don't need to network with her. I've already gotten a few books published."

I paused and gave her my full attention. "You have? That's great. And why haven't you said anything? I'll search your name later today and check them out."

She snorted, pivoting toward the door. Before she left, she looked at me over her shoulder. "You won't find anything. They're under a pen name."

That was weird. I guessed I wouldn't buy her books, then. I shrugged, remembering she was always crabby when I relieved her from the early-morning Sunday shift. I wasn't going to read too much into her flippant behavior. She was a good friend but had a tendency to run hot and cold.

As Mel hurried out, I rounded the bar then set Ava's cup on her table. Her fingers stilled on the keys, and she glanced at me with a ready smile. I was relieved when she didn't immediately mention Mel—I worried that she could have caught part of our conversation.

Ava reached for the steaming brew then took a hearty sip. "That's so much better. I don't know why that one"—she absently waved in Chloe's direction—"cannot follow instructions."

Rather than fuel that particular fire, I tapped my finger on the cover of a book to the left of her laptop. "What's this?" The title, *The Spider's Prey* by C. Marx, looked intriguing and wasn't like anything I usually saw her with. The cover was burnt orange with a silhouette of a woman running away in the background. Layered over the two was a glistening silver spider web with drops of blood clinging to several intricate strands.

"That's my guilty pleasure. Melanie recommended this author, and I'm so glad she did. I can't get enough of her books."

"Really?" I picked it up and flipped it over to read the blurb on the back. It was a psychological thriller, and after reading what it was about, I, too, was intrigued. If Melanie and Ava liked it so much, maybe I would check it out.

"The author is brilliant. And it's a great break from the boring stuff I write." She grabbed the book and attempted to stuff it into her oversized bag. "I have too much work to do. I shouldn't even tempt myself with this."

The leather satchel slipped, dangling precariously on the edge of the chair, and a few things fell out. I bent down and picked up her sunglasses. "These are nice." They were Gucci, and I could tell they were real. I didn't buy expensive sunglasses —they were too easy to lose or damage. "Oh, there's a scratch on the edge of the lens. I hope that didn't just happen."

"No, I've had them forever." She took them from my hand and shoved them into an inside pocket, got the book in, then set the bag securely on the chair next to her. Once that was done, she smiled. "Tight deadline and too much coffee. It's making me jittery."

Ava wrote nonfiction, so I could see the appeal of the thriller, especially as it got her out of the academic world she typically existed in.

One of our regulars stepped up to the counter, and I rushed back to get them what they needed before Jeffrey could emerge from the back office and catch me chatting on the floor.

Bells chimed as the door to the Coffee Hut swung open, bringing with it a rush of Hawaiian humidity. I finished taking payment from another regular then glanced at the person who'd entered. My jaw dropped as a six-foot-two hulk of a man approached. The room seemed to shrink from his presence. *Who is that?*

————

Xander

I WOVE through people on the busy sidewalk, glad to be out of my condo. It was a beautiful day, and soon, the temperature would hit the mid-eighties. The waves were perfect for surfing, and it was taking all I had to stay on task rather than spend the day at the beach, riding them. But I had other things that needed to be done, like renovating the houses on my family's private island.

I mentally checked off the things I would need to buy for the next week of work. We had four houses, one for our parents, each of my two brothers, and myself. The island was more like a family compound, but we were the only ones who labeled it that way, and our secret was well guarded.

With several weeks of time on my hands and not much else to do besides surf, I'd needed a project, and fixing up our island homes was a good one. *A girlfriend would be nice too.* But a familiar hollowness shadowed my footsteps ever since our mission had been ambushed the month before in Colombia. And I recognized the feeling as twofold—grief for those we'd lost and longing for a relationship like my parents had.

I'd never been in a relationship with a woman who I thought could be the one, like my brothers had—but they had their own problems with that. At that point in my life, I was beginning to suspect I wouldn't find someone who I couldn't live without. But I had my family, and I needed to stop thinking crazy stuff and meet up with my brother.

Jaxon was waiting for me to stop by the police station, where he was working as a beat cop for Chief Kane. They were understaffed with no one to pick up the slack, and he'd been a master-at-arms years ago. So when the police chief needed time off for surgery, he reached out and hired Jaxon. Of course, Jax said yes—he bore a boatload of guilt from when his friend, the police chief's son, had died back in high school. Someday, I hoped he would share why. Ty and I hadn't pushed him to talk. Maybe we should have.

I didn't know what exactly Jax wanted to meet about, but my guess was to see how I was doing. I rotated my shoulder, testing the tenderness around my injury. It was better, and if I hadn't had words with our new SEAL team leader, I would already be back in the fold—which was where I wanted to be.

I paused as an older man crossed my path to go into the Coffee Hut. The bell jingled overhead, and as he crossed the threshold, conversation spilled out onto the sidewalk.

All the fine hairs on my body stood at attention, as if an electrical current ran through me. A woman's sultry, sweet voice registered clearly.

Everything in me froze. As if compelled, I locked eyes with the owner of the voice and found a gorgeous woman with dark, glossy hair and a runner's slender build that looked firm but soft in all the right places. My thoughts stalled, emptied of all except her. Nothing so powerful had ever happened to me before, and I was determined to explore the unexplained connection. As the door swung back after the older man had entered, I stopped its progression and stepped inside.

She stood by a table, wearing a black apron with the Coffee Hut's logo, and chatted with a customer. Her inviting lips pulled into a smile for the blond librarian look-alike she was talking with, and the world around me faded away. I couldn't help but wonder what it would be like to experience her undivided attention, to witness her smile and her laugh, to feel the softness of her skin or the touch of her hand.

As she turned and walked toward the coffee bar, I took an

involuntary step forward as if an invisible thread connected us. The gentle sway of her hips urged me to follow. I caught a whiff of her perfume as I retraced her path to the counter. I had to meet her.

In the distance, I registered the sounds of people talking. The rich scent of the coffee added to the cozy atmosphere. At the register, I stopped. There was no one else in line, and I stood before her. She was more beautiful than I'd first thought. Whiskey-colored eyes met mine, and at that moment, I knew my world would never be the same.

———

Riley

HEAT STAINED my cheeks as our gazes locked. I snapped my mouth shut and feigned disinterest when I was anything but that. Tall, with broad shoulders quite possibly chiseled from stone, the man halted at the counter where I was, power telegraphed in his every move. But that wasn't what drew my attention to him. It was the easy grin that curved his too-kiss-able lips.

I cleared my throat, wondering where the hell that thought had come from. Guilt slammed into me after the instant pull to the stranger. I had a boyfriend who I was attracted to. We had history. I took a steadying breath and plastered a strained smile on my face.

With Chloe busy cleaning up the empties around the room, I was left to take the hot customer's order. I wasn't sure that was such a good idea. Strength emanated from him, something almost like a magnetic pull. I wasn't the only one who noticed. Several women and a few men had followed his progress from the door to the counter.

"What can I get you?" Good. My voice was friendly but not overly so.

"Coffee."

My brows rose in question. "Did you want anything else?" I waited and ignored how hearing his deep voice had felt like a full-body caress. Silence stretched between us, and I shifted from foot to foot under the weight of his stare.

"Nope. Just black and to go." His head tilted to the side, and his grin widened, flashing straight white teeth. "Unless you have a break coming up. Then I'll have it here, so long as you join me."

The heat became an inferno on my face. "I don't have a break. Just got here myself." Wow, that was intelligent. I did a mental eye roll. Stepping away from the counter, I busied myself with getting his to-go cup. The couple of minutes away from his intensity helped me to calm the hell down.

"That's on the house," Jeffrey called as he came out from the tiny back room.

"Thanks, man," Black Coffee said then turned his sinfully sexy smile my way. "I'll be seeing you around."

He'd said it to Jeffrey but had locked his gaze with mine. I couldn't move until he turned away then walked out the door. *Holy hell, who was that guy?*

Jeffrey knew. I busied myself by wiping down the already clean counter behind the bar and—in spite of not wanting him to suspect I was interested, because I wasn't; I was just curious. "You know him?"

"I went to school with Xander, so yeah, you could say that. He and his brothers were always at parties, surfing, or playing sports. I thought he would've gone pro, but he followed in his dad's footsteps and went into the Navy. He hasn't been around for a while. Probably on assignment. Since he's in the military, we comp his coffee. Same with his brothers, if they're ever in." Jeffrey turned his attention to Chloe, who precariously balanced a tray full of empties, and he rushed to help her. The crush he had on my coworker was amusing to watch. She was so bubbly and sweet that I didn't think she had a clue how he felt. He took the tray from her, and they got to work loading up the dishwasher in the back.

I scanned the small room, the cozy armchairs set off along the sides of the walls, and the wood-and-metal four-tops that filled the center. It was a busy morning. Ava waved from her usual spot in one of the corners. With no one coming through the door, I made my way over to her to chat.

"Who's the hunk?" Her blue eyes sparkled with mischief.

I took in her ever-present low ponytail, which wasn't much different from her other hairstyle of a tight bun, and couldn't help compare it to the messy bun I'd hastily twisted on top of my head after the craptastic morning I'd had. We got along well, despite the vast differences in our personalities. It was apparent in everything about us, from her neat business casual attire, her professional hairstyle that was never out of place, and her tasteful makeup. My face was bare, aside from a light coat of moisturizing lip balm.

Does Xander have a type? Ava made me wonder, as being around her with her sexy-librarian style sometimes made me feel invisible, and I couldn't help but think he would have flashed that incredible smile her way if he'd noticed her first.

"Riley." Ava waved her hand in front of my face.

"Oh." I felt myself blush. I needed to snap out of it. "I don't know him. Haven't met him before. Jeffrey went to school with him."

She pursed her lips and scanned my face. "Well, if the advisor doesn't work out, go for that guy."

3

RILEY

My muscles ached as I trudged up the stairs to my one-bedroom rental. A double early-morning shift at the Coffee Hut hadn't been the smartest thing after running ten miles as if someone had been chasing me the night before. But the breakneck pace I'd maintained had helped me to momentarily forget, in addition to providing a Band-Aid fix. The truth of the matter was that I couldn't run away from my problems quickly enough. They would always be there, lurking.

I'd fallen asleep after my shift the day before and had another nightmare. Dreams were a gift—or a curse—from the subconscious. They were supposed to rehash the events of the day or the past or foretell what was yet to come. That was what my theory class had discussed recently, in far more depth than I would have liked. The dream had left me exhausted and raw, even if I couldn't remember it—something I was sure was a blessing. So I ran on the beach nearby, as I usually did to keep the darkness at bay.

With a slight tug, I freed my hair from the tight ponytail I'd worn for work. My scalp ached, foretelling the headache I would get if I didn't pull the restrictive band out. I finger combed my long hair then let it settle in a dark mass around my shoulders, grateful once the tension eased.

Even as tired as I was, I couldn't stay cooped up inside. After washing my face and changing, I made my way out of my apartment and briskly walked to the area in town by my work.

Where are you, Ava? I shoved my phone into my pocket after almost colliding with a man staring at his screen. Midday on a Monday in Honolulu meant there were enough people on the sidewalks to make it imperative that I kept my head up rather than spam text Ava to try to get her to meet me for lunch.

After the argument with my boyfriend, Charles, I needed to talk to her. The week was shaping up to be rather difficult, and I didn't want to be alone with my thoughts. I couldn't shake the sense of impending disaster that shadowed my steps despite the sunny day. It was one of those times when I was sure I was cursed. *Are there signs that I'm oblivious to?*

A warm, salty breeze tangled my hair in front of my face, and I shoved the dark strands back then picked up my pace to the hardware store that was two buildings away from the Coffee Hut. I could have called the landlord—who could have passed as a hundred years old, rather than his self-proclaimed seventy-five—to fix the broken ceiling-fan chain, but I wanted it done right away, not in a week.

With a shove, I pushed open the door to the hardware store then slammed into a person who felt more like a brick wall. I stumbled back from the impact. His hand curled around my elbow and steadied me. Pings of awareness shot through me at his touch, and I gasped, pulling my arm away. I glanced up and to meet amiable dark-brown eyes.

My face burned as I recognized who I'd clumsily run into— Xander. "Sorry. I wasn't paying attention." I sidestepped around him, but he turned as I did, so our connection wasn't severed as I'd planned.

"Riley from the Coffee Hut." Xander grinned.

"Yep, the one and only." *I did not just say that. Could I be more awkward?*

"I'd hoped to run into you again, but I didn't expect it to be so soon." He eased back, creating some necessary space between us. "What're you here for?"

"Grad school."

"I meant this store, but that's good to know too."

I wanted to smack myself in the forehead. Honestly, I would have thought it was weird to run into him, as Honolulu was such a large city, but the hardware store was only a few buildings away from the Coffee Hut. "I came for a pull cord. I yanked on the one for the fan in my apartment a little too hard." I took another step away, getting ready to turn and flee. There was seriously too much eye contact going on, and something about the guy heightened, well, everything. Not in a bad way, but it was a lot to deal with. I wanted to deny the attraction, because I was with someone else. It wouldn't go anywhere despite the clear interest in his gaze.

My stomach chose that moment to growl. Loudly. I closed my eyes and took a deep breath through my nose before opening them. The day needed to end.

Xander chuckled. "I was going to head over to the Crab Shack. Want to come with?"

"Oh"—*is he asking me out?*—"I-I have a boyfriend." I wanted the floor to swallow me. *This is why I have one friend.*

"It doesn't have to be a date, just lunch. I could use the company."

I thought about it for two whole seconds before my stomach won. It would be nice to talk to Xander since I couldn't get a hold of Ava. Charles was teaching a class but was going to try to swing by later. "Okay, that sounds good. Should I meet you there?"

"We can walk over together. I should be done loading some stuff on my truck by then. I'll be out front when you're ready."

I nodded then left to get my pull chain as he headed out the door. It didn't take long, and I found myself hurrying to meet Xander outside. It was a beautiful day, and I needed some company—when I went back home, I had work to get done for class. Aside from a short visit from Charles, it would be a long night alone.

"All set?" Xander was leaning against a black F-150.

"Yep." I held up my small bag then turned in the direction of the restaurant, since we were walking there. He fell into step beside me, and I wracked my brain for something to talk about. Next to him, I felt small. He moved with the grace of an athlete, and despite the easy silence between us, I was glad when we reached our destination. "I've been wanting to try this place."

"It's always packed here. They serve some of the best seafood on the island. When I'm home, I eat here about twice a week."

The sign said to seat ourselves, so we claimed a table near the edge of the outdoor patio section. "Do you have a place close by?" With his dark hair and eyes and bronzed skin, he looked like a native Hawaiian. I toyed with the hem of my shirt, releasing it when the waitress dropped off menus and water before hurrying to take an order at another table.

"I do, and I have some time. I'm doing work on the cabins my family owns."

"Here on Honolulu?"

"No, it's a small private island that's been in my mom's side of the family for decades. It's about a fifteen-minute boat ride from the harbor."

Wow, his mom must come from serious money.

"What about you? Are you planning on staying here after you graduate?"

Wasn't that the question of the day. "I want to. It's gorgeous here, but I haven't made any firm plans."

"I can tell you that this place is hard to leave. A bit of paradise, and the people are pretty great. Most of them."

Our conversation came to an abrupt halt as the waitress stopped back and took our orders.

"What are you going for in grad school?" he asked.

"My MFA in photography. I've been working in the field for years but needed a change. Moving here and going to school seemed like just the thing."

"What sort of a change? Career or location?"

"I love what I do—it's not that. College was an escape for me. I needed somewhere to go and couldn't get out of Illinois fast enough. After graduating, I'd already secured representation at a couple of galleries, but I was restless. So when I ran into a college friend who mentioned that one of my photography idols would be teaching a limited-time class at a graduate college I was looking at, I was hooked. I wanted to expand what I'd learned, and he uses many of the methods I gravitate toward. It seemed like fate had intervened, so I applied, got accepted, and moved here."

What I hadn't planned on or thought would happen was falling for a very persistent psych professor, whom I'd met when Melanie, my coworker and fellow grad student, who urged me to take a couple of his classes. She was a big fan of more than his classes. She'd confided in me that they'd dated, and she wasn't the only one. But Charles swore he'd broken it off with his other girlfriends. I, on the other hand, tried to keep my relationship with him a secret.

In the beginning, I'd taken his class because it never hurt to gain knowledge, and psychology would help me to understand and interact with people better.

Xander tilted his head to the side. "You don't seem satisfied. Was it not worth the move?"

"I didn't say that." But he was partially right.

He chuckled. "You didn't have to. Your thoughts are written all over your face."

"And what thoughts were those, exactly?" I tapped my finger

against my leg, nervous about what he'd read from my expression.

"You frowned and shifted in your seat, and your napkin has been crumpled and smoothed a few times. I guessed you were restless. Dissatisfied."

I forced myself to still and didn't respond. He was right. I couldn't put my finger on exactly what was bothering me or if it was one thing or an accumulation of many, but it was there regardless.

Our food was placed in front of us, and we took a few minutes to dig in, which gave me time to think about why I wasn't all the way settled in Hawaii. He didn't push me, and as my stomach filled up with crab cakes, the tension that always developed in my shoulders when I thought about what was next in my life eased.

Even so, I shrugged. I didn't know, not really. "I have a few weeks left before graduation." I couldn't help but think about Charles and where our relationship would be then. "So we'll see. I don't have any firm plans yet. Jeffrey said you were in the military. Are you active duty?"

"Yes, but my team recently came back from a mission, and we have a short break." He took a sip of his ice water.

"Do you like it?" I couldn't imagine being in the military, but I respected those who were. It couldn't have been easy.

"I do." He polished off another soft-shelled crab.

I suppressed a shudder—I had no idea how anyone ate those.

"My dad was a SEAL, and it seemed natural for my brothers and me to follow in his footsteps. My oldest brother got out, but he lives here on the island. What about you? Do you have any family nearby?"

I ducked my head. If he could read me so easily, my response wasn't something I wanted him to see. I didn't have the best childhood. "No. My last living relative died the summer before I went into college."

"I'm sorry to hear that. You must miss your family."

His gaze burned into me, and I lifted my chin, letting go of the shield I liked to erect whenever someone asked about my past. "You would think that, but it's not bad. I got used to people leaving at an early age. My parents died when I was young, and my aunt raised me. Reluctantly. She didn't want to have children and lived alone. I was more of an inconvenience, but at least I had a roof over my head." I shrugged again. "It could have been worse."

"There are all kinds of people." He sighed, and I saw shadows pass through his brown eyes. "Is that why you're not sure about living here after you graduate? Because of feeling displaced?"

I laughed. "You read between the lines well. And yeah, I think that could be part of it. I do love the island, though. It fills my soul, my creative well."

"It'll do that. When I come back from a particularly difficult mission, this place"—he scanned the area, and a small smile curved his lips—"goes a long way in healing whatever I'm struggling with."

The plate in front of him was empty, and the restaurant's efficient waitstaff swept in and cleared it away. I still had most of my fries left, but the crab cake was pretty darn amazing, and I'd polished it off. I pushed my plate between us. "Help yourself. I can never finish the fries."

He reached for one at the same time as I did. Our hands brushed, and I snatched mine back. A sexy-as-hell smirk curved his lips, and heat climbed my cheeks. I didn't understand the tingles that erupted when we touched. The heightened awareness was a new experience and had to be because of how he looked. All that muscle, height, and dark swirl of ink on his bicep was a heady combination, without even considering how gorgeous he was.

I was used to Charles. As a theory professor and my advisor, he had his own appeal, but he was nothing like Xander. Even so, my mind flashed back to a recent conversation I'd had with Charles, and I let my mind wander.

"Riley," Charles had said, pushing his wire-frame glasses higher on the bridge of his aristocratic nose and letting a smile curve his lips. "You're looking beautiful. How did I get so lucky to have you as my girlfriend?"

Pleasure had soared through me at his words. He said sweet things to me often, and I winked at him to add some levity. "Relentless pursuit."

Laughter had filled his office, and he motioned me closer. "Worth every groveling minute of it."

I'd smiled fondly, clinging to the moments we'd shared a few days before. His mischievous smile and ready laugh had drawn me to him in the beginning. He'd helped me acclimate and convinced me that I was unique and worthy. My confidence had soared at his validation over me as an independent woman, not just an artist. As our relationship grew and deepened, other characteristics came to light, such as jealousy and a quick temper. One mistake with getting caught could topple the shaky ground that our relationship rested on.

Charles had already had an informal chat with his boss over dating several graduate students he advised, regardless of the fact that they were over twenty-one. But that was over, aside from us. We'd been together for some time, and I wanted to give our relationship more of a chance and see if it led anywhere. The kindness he'd shown me, then the love, wasn't something I was willing to discard over a few disagreements, despite the rocky interactions we'd been having lately.

I started as the waitress suddenly appeared and cleared the rest of our dishes. Xander watched me with that penetrating gaze, and I shifted in my seat. "Sorry. I've got a lot on my mind with schoolwork I need to finish today."

"No need to apologize. I'll get the check, and we can get going."

I tried to pay, but he graciously declined my offer, flagged the waitress, and took care of the bill. We stood, and I wracked my brain for something else to talk about before we parted ways. I didn't want to leave, even if I had to.

"Jeffrey told me you surfed, and that he thought you would have gone pro. Do you still get out there?"

Xander chuckled. "I don't know about going pro, but yeah, I love it. But I'm glad I went in the direction I did. It was the right thing for me to do at the time."

"When I first moved here, I took surfing lessons. It's fun."

"Maybe we could hit the beach together sometime."

"I'd like that." I genuinely meant it.

I turned down Xander's offer of a ride back to my apartment, even though his truck was only a few blocks away at the hardware store. It was a lovely afternoon, and I wanted to be outside for a while longer until I had to spend the rest of the day and evening working on a paper and my graduate project.

I had a theory objectives class, where analysis and application over the history of photography was examined and applied, then business marketing, history, and theory class, which explored the intricacies of people, environments, and emotions. And finally, I had my image, printing, and learning outcomes class that semester, and then I was done.

Photography work, portfolios, or anything of that sort, I was all over. The hours flew by. But anything else was torture. I didn't enjoy studying for Charles's theory class. While the content and discussions were interesting, the reading put me to sleep. Thankfully, I'd turned in the crazy-long paper that was due, the final one for the year. It was last minute, of course, and I hoped Charles got it in time for it to count. All that was left was a quiz and test.

Lunch with Xander had been a luxury, and I looked forward to meeting with Charles for an hour or two after his last class. I glanced at the time on my phone. He would be at my place in half an hour. As I picked up my pace so I wouldn't be late, my phone pinged with a text. My heart sank at what Charles wrote: *I won't be able to swing by today. Let's plan on tomorrow. Miss you.*

There was no explanation for why he was canceling, and irritation swirled in my gut. I missed him, too, which had been one of the things we'd argued about that morning—we wanted to spend more time together but couldn't figure out a way, given his work commitments and our need to stay on the down low so he didn't get in trouble for dating another of his advisees.

I replied: *Did you get my paper on time?*

Not to worry, it will be an A, his return text said.

That's not what I asked, I typed then deleted. My fingers flew over the keys in angry strokes. I couldn't help it. I was upset about more than his offhanded comment. *That A better be on merit and not because we're sleeping together.*

Relax, his reply said. *I'll see you tomorrow. Come to my office after class.*

No one in history had ever relaxed when told to, and it wasn't going to start with me. I shut my phone off before I said something nasty. He didn't deserve it, not really. We were both missing each other and lashing out in frustration. After several deep breaths, I managed to regain a level of calm, despite the shitstorm I had no doubt would follow my refusal to reply to his text.

4

RILEY

With about half an hour until I was to meet Ava for shopping, I entered the stairwell to jog up to the third floor. I wiped the perspiration from my forehead. Monday was officially behind me, but after morning classes today, the temperature was creeping into the mid-eighties, and I had to exchange jeans for shorts and drop off my heavy book bag. As the metal door slammed behind me and I started the climb, my cell rang. Distracted, I answered without checking to see who it was.

"Where are you?" Charles snapped.

I paused halfway up the first flight of stairs. "What are you talking about?"

"You were supposed to come to my office. I've been here for twenty minutes, and you haven't shown. I have another ten before my next class. Hurry up and get here."

For sex—that was all he wanted. He'd canceled again the night before and wanted to reschedule for today, but I hadn't responded. I was still upset about his comment about my paper being an automatic A.

Hurt and frustration curdled in my stomach, and I resumed

my trek up the stairs. We had fallen into a pattern lately that left me feeling hollow and empty. It wasn't how things had been between us a couple of weeks before, and I missed that. I didn't need to deal with his bad behavior. "I never said I was coming. After you ditched me last night, you demanded that I meet you today."

A heavy sigh filled the line, and I could picture the look of annoyance and disappointment on his face. For once, I was glad I wasn't there to see it.

"Riley, we've been over this too many times. I'm swamped. On top of my classes, grading assignments, and the incessant lawyer meetings because of my ex-wife and our continued collaboration on professional papers, my time is limited."

I'd heard it all before. Part of me sympathized with him. He did have a lot on his plate. But he wasn't the only one, and he was being selfish and taking advantage of me. "I understand you have a full schedule, but it's not only that—"

"You have no idea what it's been like with my ex. The papers were—and are—in both our names, but she screwed me. I'm a footnote." His voice rose. "A fucking footnote. I'm an expert on the subjects. Not her."

"I get that you're upset, but this is not what our issues are about."

"They have a huge bearing on my availability."

I stifled my growl of frustration at him not listening to me and paused on the landing that led to the third floor to make my point. "You have very little time for me. What you do have is based on your needs, and we meet in your office or my apartment. I've never been to your place. Nor have you taken me out on a date recently." I understood why he didn't want to go anywhere local. I was his student, and he worried about his career. I did too. But there were other places we could go. Things felt stalled and complacent.

We'd gone to several romantic settings that I loved, but I

wanted to try some nearby restaurants with him, off-the-beaten-path locations that wouldn't be a big risk. He showed no interest. He'd eaten at several of them many times, and he would claim my suggestion wasn't to his liking or he was tired of the place. His lack of willingness to indulge me was bothersome.

"What do you want from me, Riley? I'm trying, and I feel as though you're not."

God, he could be so self-centered. "You're only trying on your terms." I struggled not to shout. He would use that against me. I hated to argue. My heart hurt. We'd talked about marriage, and that was part of the reason I continued to hang in there. I'd put so much time and effort into making the relationship work, but I couldn't do it alone.

Xander flashed in my mind, stunning me for a half a second. I gritted my teeth and pushed on. It wasn't because I'd met someone new. It was because things weren't working with Charles. No one else had anything to do with that. "I like spending time with you at my place, but it's not enough. I want more. And if you can't give it to me, then maybe this isn't going to work."

"Don't give me that, Riley. It's one instance. We'll talk at your place. I'll be there after my last class."

"I can't. I'm meeting a friend and going shopping."

"That's where your priorities are? You complain to me about not making time, yet when I make an effort, you have an excuse."

I couldn't argue anymore. Silence stretched between us while I jogged up the last couple of stairs, shoved open the heavy door to my floor, then rounded the corner to my apartment. Hand on the knob, I wedged my cell between my shoulder and ear. Swinging my backpack around, I unzipped the pocket for my keys, but just the slight pressure from my hand caused the door to swing wide open. My heart pounded, and my hands tingled. It was unlocked. "Oh God."

"What?" Charles's voice sharpened.

"The door to my apartment was open." I lowered my voice to a whisper. "What if someone's inside?" I had never been so glad to be on the phone as I was in that moment.

"You must have forgotten to lock it, but I'll stay on the phone while you check."

His strained tone ignited my temper. "I don't want to inconvenience you," I snapped, completely affronted by his offhanded passive-aggressive response. Where the hell was his concern for my well-being?

"I have about two minutes until I have to leave, Riley."

It took about half a second for me to decide if I should even go in. I let my pack slide back around and gripped my phone like a lifeline. I didn't even care that he was acting like an ass. I needed him on the line to call 911 if there was someone in my apartment.

I crept closer with my heart pounding against my rib cage. Silence greeted me. Nothing jumped out as I pushed the door farther open. I didn't enter yet. My gaze scanned every inch of the living room. I could see the small kitchen off in the corner. Everything was in its place, from what I could tell. Light spilled across the rooms from the windows. *Did I forget to lock the door?*

"Well?"

I jumped. I'd forgotten Charles was still there. "It looks okay."

"Good. I've got to go to class, but I'll stop by later tonight."

I disconnected the call and worried my lower lip. *Do I even want him to?* I did a quick check of my bedroom and the bathroom, even looking in the closet, under the bed, and in the shower.

Maybe I had left it unlocked. I'd been in a hurry that morning. I'd overslept and had to rush around to get out the door in time.

After dropping my book bag on my bed, changing, and transferring a few things into my purse, I left, making sure to lock up. Goose bumps took permanent residence on my arms. Everything seemed to be in its place, but I couldn't shake the nagging sensation that someone else had been inside my apartment.

I jumped as my phone pinged with a text from Ava. She was already downtown. Shaking off my concern, I hurried out of the almost-oceanfront building and walked the few short blocks to meet her. It didn't take long before I spotted Ava's signature blond bun and her perfectly pressed clothes. I grimaced. She always appeared so put together, while I looked like I'd just rolled out of bed or had spent the day on the beach. I lifted my hand and waved as she turned to me with a smile on her face.

She stood from the bench where she waited and gave me a quick squeeze. "You look stressed. Is there trouble in paradise? Is that professor giving you a hard time?"

I shook my head. "That obvious?"

We fell into step, and she pointed to the boutique we'd planned to visit. "Let's go there and get some shopping in. Then we can have lunch at the café across the street, and you can tell me all about it." She winked.

"I could use some retail therapy." It was better than actual therapy—I wasn't much of a fan of that.

The jingle over the door alerted the salesperson to our entrance. After giving the two of us a quick scan, she headed straight to Ava, who oozed money. They started chatting about what she was looking for, and I made my escape to the clearance rack. I could've bought whatever I wanted. My income from the gallery enabled me to do that and live comfortably, but I liked finding deals on clothes. It was something that'd stayed with me after living with my aunt. I didn't want for much, but I didn't have a lot, either.

I found a long, beautiful, plum-colored skirt that flowed around my legs like a cloud. Paired with a black spaghetti-strap top, I knew it would become one of my favorite outfits. I had strappy sandals and a long turquoise-pendant necklace I could wear with it. Artsy and comfortable—my go-to style.

After our purchases were bought and packaged, we headed to eat at the outdoor patio of the café Ava had mentioned. The waiter came to take our orders, and after he set down our drinks, I leaned back into my chair and sipped on my iced tea. "Did you make your deadline?"

"Yes." She laughed, and her blue eyes sparkled. "It was tight, but I got it turned into editing on time. I have a small window before I have to start researching for the next installment, and then a meeting with a new client for some procedural manuscript they want. But that's what today is about, celebrating handing off that monumental pain." She pursed her lips. "Enough about me. Tell me what happened with you and the professor."

I grimaced again. *Is he still my boyfriend? Do I want him to be?* Lately, staying with him and working through our problems, versus throwing in the towel, had been at war in my mind. I wasn't entirely sure. We had history that was worth salvaging, but the unfortunate relationships my mom and aunt endured made me afraid to try with Charles. "Nothing new. He's being demanding of my time and I..." *I what?* "I don't know. Maybe I'm selfish."

"Look." Ava grimaced. "I don't know what you're referencing here, but we all make compromises for our significant others, within reason. Speaking as a married woman, I can tell you that no relationship is perfect. There are always ups and downs."

"I get that, I do. It's just that he's been almost callous in the way he treats me. At first, he pursued me like crazy. It was a little off-putting."

"So he was relentless, and you couldn't resist him?" Ava stirred Splenda into her coffee. "And now that he's got you, some of the magic is gone?"

"Something like that." I took another sip of tea. "It was fun. I mean, he was serious about his career, so we were careful, as I'm in one of his classes, and he's my advisor, but when we were alone, he listened to me. We would spend hours talking and laughing. I thought we had more than what it seems like we do. He'd even mentioned marriage." I didn't see the point about telling Ava about his prior girlfriends or the details about the threat to his career.

"What are you going to do?"

"I don't know yet." It was hard to let go of the feelings I had for him or of what we could have had.

"Is that why you tried to get in touch yesterday?" Ava brushed back a hair that dared to come loose behind her ear. "I'm sorry about not answering. It was too late last night for me to return your texts when I came up from the writing cave and saw them."

I waved her concern away. "It was, but I'm fine. I'm not making any rash decisions yet."

Our food arrived, and we fell silent until the waiter left.

A rush of warmth came over me, and I smiled at Ava. "I'm so glad we met." It made things easier, having someone to talk with and do something with. I was used to being a bit of a loner, but having a good friend made a huge difference, compared to what my life had been like in Chicago. There, I'd focused on getting my degree and succeeding. I didn't have time for a social life of any sort. Things felt more established for me in Hawaii, and I could take time away from school and my work.

Chloe from work and Melanie from school were also

friends, but they were a bit younger. Mel and I hung out, but I couldn't talk to her about Charles.

"I'm glad we met too." Ava's eyes sparkled. "If I hadn't switched coffee shops, I don't know if our paths would have crossed."

She used to go to the Java Stop, which was bigger than ours. They also had better seating for the couple of times a week she went to write for hours. I tilted my head and voiced what I was thinking. "Why did you switch?"

"The atmosphere there changed, and I found I couldn't get any work done."

I set my sandwich down, perplexed by her comment. "What do you mean? They're busy, and whenever I've passed by, I haven't noticed anything odd."

"One of the baristas went missing." She leaned back in her chair, nibbling on a cucumber slice. "Eventually, she was found but not in the same condition. There was something about a shoe floating in the ocean. Her shoe. It washed ashore, I believe. Since it looked like her ankle had been gnawed on by a shark, they ruled out foul play."

I shuddered at the image she portrayed. "Her foot washed up here, still in her shoe?"

Ava nodded.

I frowned. "I can see why you don't go there anymore."

"It was depressing, and the dry material I write didn't help. But all that led me to you." She smiled then shrugged.

My stomach was queasy after her story, and I pushed what was left of my food away. That wasn't something I ever wanted to find in the ocean.

Although I was glad we'd found one another, and I knew one most likely didn't have to do with the other, the story of the bodiless foot added to the sense of impending doom that had been growing since finding my apartment unlocked.

5

XANDER

The musty scent of pine and chemicals was thick in the air as Jaxon and I stood in the hardware store, vacillating between two bathroom vanities. Neither of us wanted to do it, but he needed to pick one so it could be ordered.

There wasn't anyone in the aisle, and Jaxon questioned my lack of tact regarding getting booted off base for the remainder of the month. It wasn't like me, but neither were the extenuating circumstances.

"What aren't you telling me?" Jaxon dug deeper.

"Not much. No one trusts him." We were talking about Daryl again.

Jaxon blew out a breath. "That's a problem."

"Tell me about it." I should have clarified that no one trusted him on a personal level, not skill-wise. But he knew what I'd meant.

There were many changes we'd had to get used to after the mission before the last one. Losing our team leader, John, wasn't the only blow we'd taken. Jaxon had been a huge loss, too, but at least he was alive. I'd take that over spending another term serving on Team 9 with him.

"He isn't John."

"I know damn well that Daryl isn't John." The closed expression on Jaxon's face only pissed me off further. He was doing his big-brother thing, and I knew why. He felt helpless, and the only way he thought he could make things easier was to do the fall-in-line-sailor act. When I thought I could control myself, I tried to explain again what I'd experienced. Despite how much Jaxon annoyed me, he was strategically brilliant.

"John was an exceptional leader. The problem isn't that Daryl's methods are different. It's that he lets his ego get in the way. He's standoffish, and we don't know what's in his head—case in point, the op switch-up at the last minute. The only reason we're able to have any level of success as a unit is that the rest of us have worked together for so many years. There's trust there. You know that. But there is none when it comes to Daryl or his decisions."

Jaxon narrowed his eyes, his stiff posture radiating suppressed authority. "What exactly are you insinuating here?" What I was voicing could have caused problems, and he knew it. "What are you or the team going to do based on observations with Daryl?"

I ran my hands through my hair. "I don't know. Something doesn't feel right."

Jaxon tilted his head. "Have you and Tyler talked about this?"

The youngest in our family was scarily perceptive. There wasn't anything he couldn't figure out. "Not in detail, but he was there when I confronted Daryl. Ty's frustrated too." I shrugged. "Aside from the personal stuff, it's not something I can put my finger on, but I'm worried about fatalities, not just the usual risks we signed up for." Daryl couldn't climb the ladder on fatalities and failed missions, but something smelled funny.

"Could the reaction you have to him be based on how he stole your girlfriend?"

"Possibly, but that last mission—"

"Yeah, I know."

"It's eerily similar to the one where you were injured, where John died."

Jaxon cleared his throat, his face an impenetrable mask. "I don't see the connection with Daryl. We're dealing with war-torn areas of Venezuela and Colombia. Fatalities are likely. But —and this is the last-case scenario—if you think there's anything other than ego driving Daryl to make shitty last-minute decisions, we should look closely at his background."

I got where he was going. It would raise red flags. "What about the Gray Ghost Security connection? Those guys could quietly look into things."

Jaxon nodded. "Yeah, I can make a call, but let's talk with Tyler first."

He was right. While my intuition was good, Tyler's was exceptional. We needed a change of subject. Our conversation wasn't going to resolve the loss of lives.

"How are you liking working as a beat cop?"

A familiar crooked grin stretched across Jaxon's mouth, identical to mine and Tyler's. "It's different. I'm not policing our own, but I miss being a part of a team."

"You're not going to stick with it when Chief Kane is back on the job?"

He shook his head. "No. I don't think this is where I want to go with the next chapter of my life. I'm liking the plan we came up with about working with Jack and the rest of the Gray Ghost guys."

It had its appeal. I wasn't sure if I wanted out of the Navy yet, but when I did, I wanted to join a group of former SEALs for rescue-and-recovery missions or whatever else they had going on. Those guys were tight. My brothers and I would fit right in.

I left my brother at the hardware store, checking out bathroom vanities. Most of the stuff I would need over the next week was already purchased and on the island. There were only a few other things that we both had to agree upon—or not. It didn't matter. We could alter whatever we wanted in our individual cabins, but I would get the majority done while he played at a job he got guilted into.

I shook my head, unable to stop the grin that spread from the thought of my big brother trapped in an office, doing paperwork or whatever he had to while helping Chief Kane. Not only that, but Kane was Kayla's dad, and I couldn't help but wonder what blowup would result if she came home and ran into Jaxon.

Jaxon had been good friends with Kayla's brother in high school. The problem had been that Jaxon had a thing for Kayla. But he'd never acted on it because of her brother, at least not to my knowledge. From what Jaxon told me, her brother would have had a coronary if he'd asked her out. And Kayla had grown to hate Jaxon. So something was bound to happen, sooner rather than later, with Chief Kane laid up and my brother stepping in for him.

The entire time I was in the store, I couldn't stop thinking about Riley and the time we'd spent together the day before. There was something about her that made me want to get to know her better. She liked to walk when she could, or at least that was the impression I'd gotten after we had lunch and she declined a ride home. I couldn't help but hope I would run into her if I was outside and close by where she worked.

Intent on helping the guys in the back load my truck with the larger purchases, I went the long way outside rather than cutting through the store. I needed some air. Jaxon was driving me nuts.

Not far from the Coffee Hut, I rounded the corner that took me to the side of the building and found a woman doubled over, coughing and gasping for breath. There was something familiar about her form... *Shit*. Sprinting forward, I dropped to my knees in front of Riley, carefully moving her long, dark hair out of the way so I could see her face. Tears dripped from her eyes. Her arms were wrapped tightly around her waist, her features pale.

"Riley. What happened?"

She gave only a fraction of an exhale, and not much air went in on the inhale. Pain pulled her features tight.

"Can you lift your arms?" She tried to straighten as her breathing normalized, but she whimpered. I slipped my arm around then helped her to stand fully and extend her arms over her head so her lungs could expand. Several seconds passed before she was able to take a full breath, and I repeated my question.

"Something hit me." She looked around, confusion knitting her brows together. "I don't know what. I was right there. Then something slammed into my stomach."

There wasn't anyone nearby. The only obstacle in her path was the park bench in front of the corner grocery store. "Could you have tripped and fallen against the back of the bench?"

After swiping the tears from her face, she shook her head, and her gaze grew wary. "No. I didn't fall."

I couldn't figure out what had happened. I smoothed her hair from her face then tucked a few strands behind her ears, unable to resist touching her. "Okay. Let me take a look?" I waited to lift the hem of her shirt until she gave me a small nod. Tan skin met my gaze, and I smoothed the back of my hand over her toned stomach where a bar of angry red had formed. I tried ignoring the silkiness of her skin as much as I could. It wasn't the time.

Something had gone down. I just wasn't sure what. Anger churned beneath the surface, and I fought to maintain a sense of calm as I asked her a question to which I hoped she would give a negative answer. "Did your boyfriend do this?"

"What?" Her head reared back, and her eyes went wide.

At her shocked expression, I was able to release some of the building fury. "I needed to make sure. Because if he had, I would have to pay him a visit."

"Oh." She reached out to touch my hand then pulled back at the lightest touch, as if shocked. "No, there isn't anything like that going on. Trust me. I wouldn't stay with him if there were."

Conviction clung to her words, and the last of my anger dissolved. "Let's sit down, then, unless you want to get your stomach checked out." It didn't look too bad, but she'd had the wind knocked out of her with a hard hit to her stomach, causing her diaphragm to spasm, and was probably sore. Even so, a fierce protectiveness rose in me, and I didn't want to let her out of my sight.

———

Riley

I SAT on the bench next to Xander and eased back, relaxing my aching abdominal muscles. Whatever slammed into me had caused me to double over so fast that I never saw what happened or who had done it. But someone had. That I was positive about.

Xander had left me long enough to survey our surroundings, go into the shop close to us to check for security footage, and see if anyone was hovering at an open window in the apartments above or around back. It hadn't taken long, thankfully.

A fragrant breeze, rich with the scent of hibiscus, lulled me even further, drying up the tears. Xander was a powerful force, and I let my guard down. With him by my side, I didn't worry about a potential attack or if I needed help. Contained energy sizzled around him, and when he was worried about me a moment ago, I swear he would have torn Charles apart with his bare hands if he had hit me. I couldn't believe Charles would do something like that, but I didn't know who would.

Even with Xander protecting me, the uneasy feeling I'd had with Ava returned. I'd known something was going to happen, and maybe that had been it. Maybe I'd subconsciously recognized ill intent from someone while we ate but hadn't recognized the source, possibly a passing stranger or a group of troubled teens. Ava and I had been pretty deep in our conversation and not paying much attention to anyone around us. Frustrated with not knowing who meant to do me harm, I worked to push my thoughts away.

Silence had stretched between Xander and me. It was comfortable, and I had to catch myself from leaning against him and resting my head on his shoulder. It would have been so easy to do.

There were no answers about what had happened to me. He hadn't found anything, the security cameras in the nearby stores were pointing away, and there was no reason for me to stay. I knew I should leave to get to work on my assignment, but I didn't want to. Instead, I took the time we seemed to have to get to know him a little more. With a half smile, I turned to him. "What are you doing in this area of town?"

His lips curved into that sexy grin, and I sucked in a breath. "I met my brother at the hardware store on his lunch break. He wanted to check out some finishes for the renovations I'm doing. Took longer than I thought. Good thing, or I wouldn't have run into you."

"I'm glad you found me. I would have been okay, I think, unless whoever did that stuck around." I repressed a shiver at the thought. I needed to get ahold of my overactive imagination.

He frowned. "Have you had any other run-ins?"

"No. Nothing like that." I huffed. "My life is rather boring."

Concern swam through his gaze, and he tucked a strand of loose hair behind my hear. "I'm heading to the island tonight, if you wanted to go with. There's another cabin beside mine that's in pretty good shape. You could spend the night there and get a change of scenery. And we could hang out."

Butterflies erupted in my stomach, and I nervously twined my fingers together. I wanted to say yes. "Oh, thanks. That sounds amazing, but I can't." I waved away his invitation, my mind turning back to the conversation with Charles. *Will he come by? Do I want him to?* "I have a project to do for school."

"Well, if you change your mind, the invitation's open. I'll be here a couple more days until I'm mostly on my family's island. But I'm only a phone call away."

We chatted for a couple more minutes. Xander insisted on walking me home, and I let him. Even though I didn't trust my reactions around him, I wanted to spend more time with him. So for the next twenty minutes, I indulged that part of me that craved his presence. When we arrived, any remaining tension eased at the locked door to my apartment.

When he said goodbye and our hands brushed, tingles shot up my arm. As my apartment door shut behind me, I couldn't deny it any longer, and guilt weighed heavily on my shoulders. I was dating Charles, but I wanted Xander.

6

RILEY

The next day, I was glad that Charles had never shown. The project I needed to do for my theory class was finished and turned in. That morning was busy at the Coffee Hut, and my shift flew by. With only one class on my schedule that day, I decided to stop in his office after he was free. I'd checked his schedule, and he had hours until his midafternoon class.

The guilt I felt from my reaction to Xander was still high, and I wanted to test how things were between Charles and me. I was confused—that had to be it. We'd been fighting more, and it was inevitable that I'd noticed Xander because, well, he was him. There was no not seeing him.

I entered the building where Charles's office was and made my way down the hall, prepared to knock on his door. It was open, but I rapped on the frame anyway. His head came up, that thick shock of sandy-blond hair fell over his forehead, and his brown eyes lit up behind the wire frames I thought looked so sexy on him. With his white button-down slightly wrinkled and his signature navy-blue tie with his alma mater's seal, I remembered what had drawn me to him—intelligence with a certain boyish charm. He had it in spades. Or at least he seemed to, with his various publications and elevated position at the university. When he'd pursued me, a part of me had been flattered.

"Riley, what a surprise." He pushed the hair back from his forehead.

I snapped out of my thoughts and smiled at him. "I thought I would stop by and see if you're free."

"I am." He stood, towering over me as he reached around to shut the door. The lock clicked into place. "I missed you."

He bent and covered my lips in a hungry kiss, and I let my backpack slip to the nearby chair as he guided me toward his desk. I lifted my arms and encircled his neck, appreciating his ardor. I'd missed him too.

The backs of my legs pressed against Charles's desk. His mouth moved over mine with more insistence, and I tried to match his enthusiasm, but something felt off. I couldn't figure out what. Threading my fingers through his hair, I relaxed into his kiss, seeking the connection we'd once had.

His hands roamed over me, insistent and hurried. He pulled the hem of my shirt up, and I let him because the blinds were closed and the door locked. We'd done the same thing before, many times. At least that was what I kept telling myself as he grew bolder and more aggressive in his touch.

My back arched as he bent me over the top of his desk. Lifting one of my legs, he ground against me then picked me up, so I was reclining over the mahogany surface. My confusion swirled at how fast he'd moved. When his fingers bit into my waist as he wrestled to get my shorts off while simultaneously kissing and touching me, unease clouded my mind, and I put a voice to it. "What're you doing?" I reared back, escaping his lips to meet his eyes.

Frustration flashed across his flushed features. "I'm sure you can figure that out, babe."

My stomach plummeted. I hated it when he called me that,

as I imagined that he used it with all his prior girlfriends. Pushing at his shoulders, I attempted to break free. He wasn't having it, too consumed to notice. "Stop. Charles!"

He froze with his hands on his belt buckle and annoyance curling his upper lip. "What? You came here. You can't be serious about not wanting to have sex with me."

My feet gained purchase on the floor. I pushed him back and skirted around him, pulling my shirt on once there was some space between us. "I came by to see you. Not have you grope me like that." I flung my arm out at his desk. "I have no idea what that was, but it wasn't about us."

Inside, I trembled. His touch had been cold, aggressive, and hurried. There was nothing about it that conveyed he was thinking about me, about us. It was desperate and, for me, stressful.

He shoved his glasses back onto his face, straightened his shirt, and adjusted his tie. "What's going on with you? Is this about needing extra attention again?"

What the hell is wrong with him? "No, Charles." I felt sick. This was not the person I'd thought he was. It was clear I'd read more into the relationship, and he'd just wanted a hookup. I guessed, despite how great it had been in the beginning, the challenge was over for him. "This isn't working out."

"Give me a break, babe." He huffed as he went around his desk and adopted that scholarly expression I'd thought I loved. "I'll come over later today, and we can talk."

His snide tone solidified my decision. I grabbed my bag, flicked the lock, and got the hell out of his office. I ignored him calling after me as I hurried down the hall. The building's door slammed behind me. Outside, I unleashed the tears I'd been holding in check, and they rolled down my face. Fumbling with the small zippered pocket on my backpack, I pulled out my sunglasses to hide my emotional turmoil. Thank God I didn't have an afternoon shift.

My steps slowed once I was off campus. I wasn't too far from my apartment and could use the walk rather than hopping the bus. I didn't care how long it took to get home. The fresh air would clear my head.

After a couple of blocks, I finally put my finger on what I was feeling—used. His touch had been detached, his eyes glazed. That hadn't been us back there. I had been a warm body only, and I had a sick feeling that I knew why. There had to be someone else who was unattainable, and he was fantasizing about her rather than me. The signs were there and increasingly so.

He'd pursued me so hard, and when I'd given in, he'd been so attentive. It was impossible not to feel special, and I'd considered myself lucky, thinking that what we had would continue to grow and evolve. But then his eye had wandered more and more. He had grown complacent. If he stopped over for a drink but didn't get what he wanted, his temperament would turn nasty. I was a possession that he felt he should have unlimited access to. The mature, caring man I'd thought I was involved with wasn't that at all. He was childish.

But it wasn't only his fault. I was guilty too. Horror filled me at the revelation. *Am I falling into the same pattern as my family?*

———

Xander

A WARM, balmy breeze stirred the outdoor hanging lights around the patio's perimeter. I tipped my beer back then flagged the waitress for another when she passed by. Ty and Jaxon arrived at the same time, pulled out chairs, and took their seats. We only waited on Mark, the analyst we worked with.

"Thanks for ordering for us," Jaxon said.

I knew what my brothers drank, but I hadn't ordered for

Mark—I didn't know him that well. He did communications analysis for the SEAL teams. I'd met him through Ty, and we'd also stood up for him a time or two when Kyle, another member of our team who was generally a dependable and great guy, had been his usual arrogant-jerk self to our support staff. "Where is Mark?

Ty twisted in his chair, looking around the beachside bar. "He should be here soon."

"Do you think it's the best idea to involve him?" Jaxon leaned forward. "That last mission didn't go well, and I can't say it didn't benefit him by making his life easier."

"He's not like that," Ty said in Mark's defense, tipping his chair so he balanced on the back legs. "He was a nerdy, quiet guy in school, and he's pretty much the same now, with the exception of having a girlfriend."

"I thought they broke up?" It wasn't a secret that Mark was dating another analyst on base. Ty had mentioned that there was some drama going on between them one day after Mark had been a distracted mess when he presented at one of our meetings. The incident was well-known.

An acoustic guitar strummed inside as a band took the stage to warm up. It was going to get loud, even on the outdoor patio. Ty and Jaxon were mumbling about something while I stared at the surf. There was a bonfire going on the beach, and a couple ran, hand in hand, into the waves, laughing and jumping rolling crests until they fell into the frothy water. I couldn't help but smile as Riley invaded my thoughts. At lunch the other day, she'd told me she'd learned to surf. I wanted to take her out. I knew she had a boyfriend, but there was an undeniable connection between us, and I hoped she would give me a chance. I didn't think her relationship would be long-term, as she didn't light up when she talked about him.

"What's that look on your face?" Ty broke into my thoughts.

"What?" My smile turned into a grin when Mark appeared.

Good timing. They'd have to let it go. Besides, I wasn't sure I wanted to share Riley with my brothers yet, at least not until I was able to take her out on a real date. "Hey, Mark. Glad you could make it."

Ty and Jaxon narrowed their eyes for a moment longer before turning their attention to Mark. They echoed similar greetings, and we waited to talk business until Mark's drink arrived.

"I told Daryl," I began, "about how Kyle took the brunt of the explosion when Daryl sent him in first. Daryl changed the plan at the last minute."

"But Daryl is the team leader. Why would he go first?" Mark asked.

"The communication came through you, Mark, but the informant asked for Daryl specifically. The connection, for whatever reason, was there. That's how they rehearsed the op, for him to take point," Ty said.

"Exactly," Jaxon added. "The informant was cartel, and they want territory. Our entire reason for getting the guns out of the Venezuelan government's hands was so that they wouldn't occupy more space on the map. That area is brewing with conflict. So why was the informant rigged with explosives? Who set the messenger up and why?"

"It's probably the Venezuelan government. It doesn't make sense for it to be anyone associated with the cartel," Mark murmured. "Besides, they could've gotten Daryl's name through other connections, possibly even a leak in the Venezuelan government."

"That'd be my guess too." I drummed my fingers on the table. The plan for tonight was to get together and have a few beers. I'd wanted to see if anything odd came up about Daryl from Mark or even Ty, but it hadn't. Either way, it was good to get out for a while with the guys.

We were about to wrap things up when Ty's eyes sparkled. I

knew where that mischievous look would lead and needed a distraction. "Mark, how are things with Anna?"

"Good." His smile broadened. "I had to attend prayer to prove I was committed to her, but that's a small sacrifice to make for having her back."

"I'm happy for you, man." Ty clapped Mark on the shoulder.

"Would Anna be willing to flag any suspicious data with Venezuela chatter that fits into what we're searching for and let you know?" Jaxon asked, bringing the conversation back to our problem.

"Yeah, I'm sure she would. I'll check with her and see if she's noticed anything that didn't seem relevant but would actually help us out." He glanced at the time on his phone. "I've got to head out. I'll let you know if I find anything."

I took the last swallow of my beer and went to get up too. "On that note, I've got to head out."

Ty's hand tightened around my arm, and a wicked grin stretched across his face. "You're not going anywhere. Tell us why you had that big goofy smile on your face."

I laughed and leaned back against my seat. "I met someone."

"Yeah?" Jaxon's gaze sharpened, and with his fingers loosely wrapped around the neck of his beer, he twirled the base on the table. "What's she like?"

"Sweet, artistic. She's got this long dark-brown hair, sexy whiskey-colored eyes, and..." I shrugged. I didn't want to go into how gorgeous she was or the fact that I wanted to kiss her for hours. Or that I could spend all day talking to her and never get bored. There was something different about her, and I intended to find out what. "I can't stop thinking about her."

7

RILEY

The pop from the cork echoed through my tiny kitchen as I pulled it from the bottle of red wine. The day had been enlightening, to say the least. With a full glass in hand, I went out to my patio. My night plans consisted of my drink, the sunset, and no complications. A mixture of burnt oranges and purples painted the sky over the hint of rolling waves from the small portion of the ocean I could see. I relaxed back against the settee, and propped my feet on the ottoman, happy to be alone.

The strain between Charles and me was more taxing than I was comfortable with, and that right there was a huge sign. Then there was the incident in town when I was hit in the stomach, and the apartment break-in. My cell pinged, startling me from my thoughts. I glanced at the screen and sucked in a shaky breath.

An unknown number had texted me. *I won't let this go.*

Maybe it was Charles. Biting my lower lip, I toyed with ignoring it, but my curiosity got the better of me. *Who is this?* I typed.

I waited. No little dots showed from someone texting back. Unease churned in my stomach along with the hearty glass of wine I'd had. I was ridiculous. It was probably a wrong number, and if it had been Charles, he was a jerk.

My frown deepened. It had to have been Charles. He didn't do well with rejection, and I bet it was his way of retaliating, trying to treat me like an errant child. I pressed the button and turned my cell off. I was done.

After several deep breaths, I let the stress of the day go. I took a few more sips while the distant roar of the ocean lulled me into a state of peace. I was minutes away from falling asleep and completely okay with that.

A loud knock at my door sent a jolt of surprise through me, and my hand jerked. Several drops of wine spilled over the edge of my glass, staining my jeans. *Dammit.*

A few seconds passed where I considered ignoring whoever was there, but the knocking persisted, getting progressively louder. Leaving my wine outside, as I fully expected to return to my chair, I went to the door and opened it. Charles leaned against the doorframe in the hallway, his dark-blond hair disheveled as if he'd run his hands through it more than once.

The academic, rumpled vibe he had going was what had drawn me in the first place. And in a way, it still did. I waited, saying nothing, my gaze briefly dropping to his ever-present navy tie.

I wanted to see how he was going to play it and if he would apologize or continue down the same condescending path he had been on for the past week. That wasn't the guy I'd fallen for.

A sad half smile curved his lips. "Can I come in?"

I shrugged but opened the door wider, barring entrance with my body. Conflicting signals, but it was how I was feeling. "It depends on why you're here."

"To apologize," Charles murmured.

In that case, yes. I stepped aside. He shuffled in then meandered over to the kitchen, where the red wine was. He opened a cabinet, took out a glass, then turned to me with the bottle in his hand. "Do you mind?"

"Help yourself."

I waited for him to take his first sip. He swirled the deep-red liquid around the glass, and legs formed on the sides before he lifted it to his lips and drank deeply. Neither of us said a word when he lowered the nearly empty glass to the counter then leaned against it, his shoulders slumping forward. "I'm sorry for pressuring you, Riley. It's been a stressful week, and I took it out on you. And I'm here to tell you that I'm not giving up on us."

That was a start, even if that last part sounded similar to a text message he'd sent earlier. "Thank you."

He lifted his head, and hope shone in his eyes. "Then I'm forgiven?"

I pursed my lips. It was complicated. "Yes, for in your office. But not for the text." *And I didn't say we would get back together.*

His brows furrowed. "Text?"

I wanted to roll my eyes at him. "Yeah. The one that said, 'I won't let this go.'"

The blood drained from his face, leaving him pale and chalky looking. "What number did that come from?" he rasped then finished off his glass of wine.

"Unknown." Weird. I'd been sure it was from him and still had doubts that it wasn't. His hand clutched his chest, and the veins on his neck stood out. *Oh no*—he didn't look well. "Charles?" I rushed forward as he slumped over. My hands fisted his shirt, helping to hold him up. "What's wrong?" I couldn't hide the hysteria as my voice climbed in pitch.

He gasped, and his knees buckled.

"Oh God!" I dug my cell from my pocket and powered it back on. "I'm calling 911."

"No." His voice was weak and breathy, and he slid to the floor.

My eyes welled in confusion as I waited for the emergency operator to pick up.

"No. You take—"

"I can't." There was no way I could get him down three flights of stairs and into his car. The operator came on the line, and I rattled off my location and his symptoms. An ambulance was on its way. *Don't die on me.* I sat beside him and held his hand. His palm was clammy, and mine shook.

It probably took less than fifteen minutes for the paramedics to arrive and get him situated and off to the hospital. I followed in Charles's car. But it felt like hours. Our relationship hadn't been perfect by a long shot, but I cared whether he lived or died. That was all I could manage to think about. The status of our relationship, the fight, took a back seat to the fear for his life. It had to have been a heart attack. Maybe he was telling the truth, and stress and pressure had been getting to him.

We weren't getting back together, but I could be more understanding and ease out of what we had together. I had to be.

The tires screeched as I pulled into a spot in the emergency room parking lot. I jumped out, pressed the key fob, and heard the beep as the car locked. I ran to the entrance, and the automatic doors slid open. As soon as I crossed the threshold and skidded to a stop at the front desk, I blurted out, "Charles Wright was brought here by ambulance. Is he okay? Can I see him?"

"And who are you in relation to him?"

I wrung my hands, settling on what would mean I could see him. "I'm his girlfriend."

The older woman typed on her keyboard, her gaze scanning the screen. "I'm sorry, dear. As you're not family, I can't disclose any information." She shrugged. "HIPAA laws."

My heart thudded against my ribs as she refused to look at me. "Well, is he okay? If he's awake, I'm sure he'll tell you to send me in. Can you ask him?" I bounced my leg, my knee knocking at the front wall of her desk.

She clicked on her keyboard for a few more strokes then sighed, her hands sliding away as her gaze met mine. "His HIPAA forms were recently updated, and I know who he is."

She'd already said something like that, but I had trouble focusing. My ears rang, and my leg jerked. "He's divorced. Maybe he listed me on there?" Something that I couldn't decipher flashed over her features.

"I can't share any medical or personal details from his chart with you. But, honey, a little word of advice from someone who knows something." Her eyes softened with what looked like pity. "He's married and not worth your time."

———

Xander

THE NIGHT SKY was filled with stars, and a cool breeze rolled off the ocean, rocking the hammock in a gentle swaying motion. It was peaceful, and I didn't want to go inside and find my bed. The waves broke against the shoreline, rhythmic and lulling, and I drifted off to sleep with Riley in the forefront in my mind. But my subconscious had other ideas the deeper I sank into sleep.

My body tensed, and the hammock shifted as sleep transported me from the peaceful beach house and dreams of Riley's soft lips to the sweltering jungle in Colombia, where our last mission had taken place. The air was thick with humidity and mosquitos, but the lack of nocturnal noise piqued my awareness. It was the first sign that all wasn't right, but it was too late in coming.

Daryl had made Kyle take point. I'd thought it was unusual, as it wasn't what we'd rehearsed. Ten more steps, and I would have been at the front door of the building. Kyle had breached the entrance with Daryl on his heels. Something was wrong. Daryl burst from the door. But Kyle wasn't out. Daryl turned with a grimace as he glanced over his shoulder. *What spooked him?*

Kyle had tried to get inside the building, which was our goal. Get in, recover the weapons, get out. The weapons were supposed to be inside.

Then all hell broke loose. The informant was rigged with C-4. We turned to retreat. The explosion rocked the night and threw us to the ground. Kyle staggered past the door with blood pouring from a deep wound on his neck before crumbling to the ground.

Kyle was down. I was hit in the shoulder. When I got him in a fireman's carry, gunshots exploded around us. The heat trail of a bullet burned the skin on my neck. *Dammit!* Daryl continued to cover us. Through night vision goggles, I sensed movement and adjusted my aim. One shot. Target hit.

From the fire we were taking, they must not have wanted us to find the weapons.

"Joe, goddammit, where are you?" We were supposed to be radio silent, but the ambush changed things.

"On your six," Joe sounded in my ear.

Joe was on high ground. We'd found a good spot for coverage in the dense jungle, and he'd set up to pick off targets. We hadn't expected so many.

Joe and Daryl covered us, and targets fell in fast succession around the perimeter of the jungle. They were far enough away from the building but close enough to fire on us even without the proper night vision gear.

Pain seared my shoulder. My eyes shot open. With my breath sawing in and out, I surveyed my surroundings, intent on taking down an enemy.

But the lack of jungle, screams, and explosions made reality descend. I was out of the hammock quickly, and sweat rolled down my neck as my gaze jerked around the empty beach.

It took a few minutes to pull myself out of the nightmare and into reality. I held still, my fists clenched at my sides, needing the weight of the weapons in my hands as my heart slowed, and my breathing grew more regulated. The flashbacks were relentless, and after each one, I had a sense that I'd missed something critical.

Calmer, I sat on the porch of my cabin rather than the hammock and slipped my cell from my pocket. I opened my contacts list and tapped my thumb on Tyler's name. It rang several times before Tyler answered and grunted a hello.

It grounded me. My younger brother could be a real pain. "That's how you answer the phone?"

"You okay?" Tyler's voice sharpened.

"Fine. Couldn't sleep."

"Is there any reason you needed to wake me to keep your pansy ass company?"

The tension in my shoulders eased somewhat, and I grinned. Of my two brothers, Ty was the one who could do that. He had a sharp wit and an even quicker instinct when it came to fighting. Having him on my team was both a blessing and a curse. "Yep. Since you don't need beauty sleep on account of your face being the way it is, I decided you should keep me company."

He chuckled. Rustling sounded then the clink of bottles. "How's your shoulder?"

I rotated my left arm, easing the soreness that his question had moved to the forefront of my mind. "It's good. Healing."

A chair creaked, and I could picture him tipping it back on two legs with that cocky-as-hell look on his face, the one he wore when he was trying to disguise what he was thinking. For most people, it worked, but not for me or our oldest brother, Jaxon. I narrowed my gaze and scanned the dark horizon, taking in a boat's blinking lights from shore. Ty had told me he'd gone over the details with Daryl from our last mission, as they were both assigned to our unit through temporary addition orders. "You sense it too?"

"Yeah." He let out a deep sigh. "That ambush was a massacre. We didn't stand a chance, and Daryl isn't saying shit."

"I want to know why." I had a bad feeling about how things had gone down and the botched recovery—our team had barely escaped. Two of our guys hadn't been so lucky. "I feel like we're missing something major. No one's looking into what went wrong?"

"No. Daryl was pissed, but nothing's been done aside from the initial investigation. We're back to square one with this shit. We may go on another tour in two weeks. Intel's trickling in."

"And that's supposed to be trusted? The messenger was wired. It was a setup."

"The Navy's calling it unlucky," Ty said with a growl. "We need to know more. I think—"

"Do it." I knew what he was going to say, and there was no sense in saying it over the line. Ty had been in the same grade as Mark, our communications analyst, in high school. We needed new eyes and ears, and with him, we stood a chance. Ty would talk Mark into looking into Daryl's personal life where he could. If he was guilty of anything, Mark would find a money trail somewhere.

"Same bloody page, brother." Ty cleared his throat. "Your contract's up soon, yeah? Have you signed for another block of time?"

That was the question—to reenlist or not. "I'm still thinking about it." I rubbed my hand over my forehead, trying to smooth away the problems. "I've got a little time before I decide."

We chatted for a few minutes longer about the island. After we hung up, that sixth sense I'd had wouldn't go away. Ty would talk to Mark and get him to look into Daryl, to dig deeper. If he was on the take, we needed to find out before more lives were lost.

I set my phone down and headed to the water. The only way I would get any sleep was if I exhausted myself, and swimming a few miles at top speed was a good way to accomplish that. We had a plan that I hoped would yield quick results.

RILEY

He's married. The knife sliced through my sandwich with more force than necessary. I was glad to be home for lunch, even if only for a short while. The news I'd received at the hospital, followed by a sleepless night, had made that morning's classes difficult. It hadn't mattered that I'd already broken up with him. I felt like such a fool.

All the times he'd made excuses about why he didn't want to go out to eat or do anything outside of his office or my apartment suddenly made sense. He didn't want to be seen with me because he was afraid we'd get caught by his wife.

I lifted the mangled sandwich and chewed. I tasted nothing. Disgusted, I shoved the plate away. In half an hour, I would leave for work. It was better that way. That was one place where I had no memories of Charles.

Pounding at my door startled me, and I jumped. My nerves were shot. I had a sinking suspicion of who was there, and resigned to get the confrontation over with, I flipped the lock and opened it wide. Charles stood in the hallway, a frown marring his handsome face.

"How are you feeling?" I could be cordial.

"Better. My heart is fine. It was a false alarm." He punctuated that with a nod. "Why weren't you there when I was released?"

I clenched my teeth, vowing not to shout my response or ask what had caused him to collapse. "I didn't want to run into your wife."

"What are you talking about?" Charles's shoulders tensed, and he took a step inside.

"I didn't invite you in." I held my ground and kept my hand on the open door, blocking him from coming inside. "And you know what I'm talking about. It seems your HIPAA papers were recently updated. The nurse let it slip that you're still married, as in not divorced. My guess is she knows your wife personally to have shared that little gem."

"She doesn't know anything." He took another step forward, crowding me.

I wasn't having it. My hand went up, palm facing him. "Do not come in. You're not welcome here." Disgusted, I shook my head. "It all makes sense now. Never wanting to go anywhere with me. I thought we avoided certain places because of worry over your career and our involvement. My guess is that your wife doesn't go to the university much." I narrowed my gaze on him. "Or ever."

"You haven't seen her there for a reason. Why, Riley, do you think that is?"

Games within games—I wasn't playing them. "As I said before, we're done, Charles. I don't want this anymore." My hand pushed against his chest, nudging him back a little so that I could shut the door. "Don't come here again."

Fury painted his face red. "You'll regret this and come crawling back."

I slammed the door in his face and slid the lock home. What an asshole. I was livid. That interaction chased away the lingering sadness over breaking up. I glanced at the time and saw that I had to get moving so I would make my shift at the Coffee Hut. My hand shook as I tossed the sandwich then put the plate in the dishwasher.

After a few calming breaths, I checked out the window to ensure his car wasn't in the parking lot. Only then did I leave, locking up behind me. It was a good thing I had several blocks to walk to work. I needed the time to cool down. As I gained some distance from my apartment, the trembling in my hands subsided, but the deep sadness I'd wrestled with over another severed relationship clung to me.

Will I ever learn? Or am I destined to have one horrible relationship after another, following in my mom and aunt's footsteps?

The weather was unusual in Honolulu for that time of day, but the slight chill in the air fit my mood. With the trade winds, we would get half an hour of rain daily, even during the dry season. Puffy clouds vied for space alongside dark, stormy ones. I hoped for a raging storm, one that lasted longer than usual. It would be slow at work, but I didn't think I could muster a smiling face for customers, anyway. Maybe Jeffrey could put me on bar instead of the register. The less interaction, the better.

The bells jingled overhead as I entered the Coffee Hut, desperately trying to swap my heavy mood for a lighter one. A familiar blond head turned my way, which was a pleasant surprise. I gave Ava a small wave then stopped at her table. "Why are you here so late in the day?" I worked mornings, most of the time, and that was when she usually came in to write.

"I'm heading out of town to California in an hour and thought I'd get some last- minute work done on this presentation before I head to the airport. What do you think?" She swung her computer toward me so I could see the screen.

The title of the seminar was bold across the top of the document, with her picture to the left and several bullet points to the right. I didn't pay attention to any of that, as I knew that wasn't what she was asking me.

"It's a good picture." I didn't want to tell her she looked stiff and unapproachable. As far as portraits went, it was fine, but it could have been better. "Do you want me to take some new ones when you're back in town?" That would be a good distraction, and I needed several of those.

Her smile was blinding. "Yes, I would love that."

"Okay. That'll be fun." I tapped my fingers on her table and inched toward the register. "I need to get working. I'll chat with you later."

Ava's soft chuckle followed me. She saw through what I wasn't saying, but that was okay. It was why we were friends. I didn't need to insult her picture.

Jeffrey took mercy on me after one look at my strained features and put me on bar, which went great until Chloe needed a bathroom break. I glanced out the large picture window across from where I stood at the register. The sky was a seething mass of dark clouds, from which fat drops of rain fell. There were a few patrons inside, mostly regulars, and with the weather what it was, I didn't expect many new customers. I was wrong when the bell chimed on the heels of that thought.

The room seemed to shrink as Xander walked in, taking up entirely too much space. I wasn't the only one to notice. Most of the women lifted their heads, interest evident in their expressions and body language. Moving like a professional athlete, he made his way to the counter, his presence packing a serious punch.

Chloe wasn't back yet from her bathroom break. It looked like I would be waiting on him. I bit down on my lip then realized what I was doing. Xander stopped in front of me and frowned.

"Are you all right?"

"Yeah." I waved away the exhaustion he must have observed from the half-moons hanging beneath my eyes. "Long night and a breakup. But I'm better for it."

He tilted his head to the side and took my measure once more. "The timing of this probably sucks, but would you want to go out to dinner tonight?"

Should I? I needed the distraction, and I was attracted to him. I let a second pass before I fired off the questions that rolled through my head. "Married?"

He chuckled. "Nope. Never have been."

"Girlfriend?"

"Not presently, but we'll see how this date goes." He grinned, and I was momentarily sidetracked.

I pursed my lips because my next question was rude, but I wanted to know. "Ever cheat?"

Anger flashed in his gaze, and the tension in my shoulders eased. "No. Not my style."

"In that case, I'm up for something, but maybe not dinner. I'm pretty tired and won't be great company." I wouldn't have blamed him if he'd changed his mind. I sounded a little crazy—or maybe just scorned.

"How about the beach? If you're not working tomorrow morning, I can pick you up early, and we'll make a day of it?"

"Which beach? Here or your island?" I wasn't ready to chance being alone in a remote location with him. I liked him and even felt safe around him, but that seemed like a little more than I could deal with.

"Here. But I'm leaving for the island on Sunday, if you want to go then."

"No, that's okay. I'm good with a beach here tomorrow."

The door chimed behind him, signaling another customer as Chloe strolled back in after her much-longer-than-necessary break. We made quick plans for him to swing by and pick me up at nine. Since I didn't have class or work, there was no reason not to go. To be honest, I was looking forward to it, relieved to be done with Charles, and determined to have fun.

Xander left with his black coffee, and Chloe grabbed my sleeve, tugging me back. "That's what I missed? I'm sorry I took so long on my break."

I raised my eyebrows at her. "I thought you were just using the bathroom."

She shrugged. "Jeffrey told me I could take a few minutes longer if I wanted. Not sure why."

"Really? It was probably so you didn't wait on that guy." Jeffrey had it bad for her, and I was sure he would have seen Xander as competition, as he hadn't even gotten up the nerve to ask Chloe out yet.

"Oh, I doubt that. It wouldn't have mattered. He's hot but too old for me. Just be glad Melanie wasn't here."

That was true. Our coworker Melanie had this weird jealous streak if we got attention from a guy she'd set her sights on. I'd recently learned she'd dated Charles, and when she'd overhead Ava say something about the advisor being my boyfriend, she'd lost her mind. We'd gotten over it enough to be civil at work, but I was a little wary around her because of it. It was sad—she was a lot of fun, and we were friends.

A customer came to the counter, and Ava stood to pack up her things. Chloe took care of the new person while I slipped around the counter to have a word with Ava before she headed out for her flight.

Her gaze caught mine, and a devious smile curved her lips. I shook my head and laughed. "We're just hanging out tomorrow. It doesn't mean anything. Besides, I got out of a relationship hours ago. I don't need to jump into a new one."

"Pfft. That hunky guy is what you need to get under and effectively get over the professor." She slung her bag over her shoulder. "I'll be back next week, and I want a full report."

As she exited the Coffee Hut, I couldn't help but think she could be right. Not about the get under part—I rolled my eyes at her retreating form—but taking a chance on something new, even if it was only to take my mind off a messy breakup, seemed like a good plan.

9

RILEY

The sun sparkled off cresting waves and sent a jolt of excitement through me at the prospect of riding them. We pulled into a parking space, and Xander turned the engine off. After he got out and shut his door, he came around to mine. With my sunglasses firmly in place, I could check him out without getting caught. He had muscles on top of muscles, and I marveled at how he moved. The tattoo on his bicep and part of his chest practically begged my fingers to run over them and trace the intricate swirls.

I was glad I'd worn a cover-up over my black bikini. Xander had on navy swim trunks with a gray stripe down the side and no shirt. It'd made for a tension-filled ride to our destination as I tried not to stare. His shoulders flexed as he lifted the surfboards from the bed of the truck and balanced them on one shoulder. In his other hand, he carried a cooler full of drinks. "Want to grab the bag in here, and I'll take these?"

I pulled my beach bag from the passenger-side floor, looped the straps over my shoulder, then pointed at the cooler. "I can carry that if you want." Or I could watch him do it. I grinned when he shook his head.

"I've got it. If you can take my bag, we're good to go."

I plucked the tan bag from the bed of the trunk and fell into step beside him. Little granules kicked up behind me, hitting my calves after each footfall. Pausing, I bent down, slipped off my flip-flops, and hooked my fingers through the straps, dangling them from my hand. The sand was cool beneath my feet, but that would change as the sun climbed the sky.

We wove through the other beachgoers then stopped midway to the shore, and Xander lowered the drinks then rested the boards in the sand. He rotated his shoulder, and I wanted to ask about the pink scar but didn't. Instead, I dropped the bags next to the cooler, took off my cover-up, and dropped it into my bag. My flip-flops went next to it, along with the shoes he'd toed off.

"I'm pretty sure you mentioned when we went to lunch that you'd surfed before, right? Or do you need a lesson?"

I let my gaze crawl over his features, wondering what his game plan was. I couldn't get a read other than him genuinely wanting to know. He focused on my eyes, and for a second, I was a little surprised. *Maybe I'm more into him than he is me?* Not once had he checked me out. Mentally, I shrugged. It was a good thing. I had to stop overanalyzing.

His brows climbed his forehead, and I realized I was staring at him but not answering his question about surfing. Embarrassed, I flashed a quick smile. "I'm not a pro, but I can hold my own."

"Great. Let's do this, then." He passed one of the boards to me, and I maneuvered it parallel to the ground and tucked it under my arm. The beach was wall-to-wall of people already, but with Xander by my side, we cut a clear path through them. We closed the distance to the water and waded in enough before lying prone on our boards.

The turquoise ocean was gorgeous and as warm as bathwater. The sun beat down on us, but I didn't mind. Side by side, we paddled out. Every once in a while, I snuck a look at him. Beads of water clung to his broad shoulders as his powerful arms flexed with each stroke.

Refocusing on why we were there, I pushed into a sitting position, letting my legs dangle on either side. Scanning the horizon, I checked for a promising wave. Xander pulled up not too far from me and did the same. It didn't take long before he pointed to a swell in the distance. "There."

"I see it." I turned and paddled toward the shore, working on picking up speed. As soon as the powerful wave neared, I dug my arms in harder then gripped the sides of the board, popped to my feet, and dropped down the vertical wall of blue water to ride the face. I balanced with one foot in front of the other and my arms extended. Worry over getting hammered slid from my thoughts during the smooth ride.

My speed increased, and my heart thundered in my ears, in harmony with the quality wave. In the pocket, the wave broke behind me. Whitewater frothed. I kept my sight on the opening of the curl.

I hunched low and cut through the barrel, and the wave crashed behind me, sending a spray of water to kiss the back of my calves.

I heard Xander roar in excitement and turned to see his fist pump in the air at my ride. I grinned then readjusted my position, so I was once more sitting on my board. I wanted to wait to paddle back out so I could watch his approach.

After about five minutes, he charged a wave. His shoulders bulged as he jolted to his feet with an ease I'd seen only on professional boarders. My breath hitched in my throat as he turned hard and surged up the face. If I hadn't been interested in him before, it would have pushed me over the edge, headfirst and diving quickly. But I already was. Watching him ride that wave made my attraction grow to impossible heights.

When he got to my side and sat astride his board, we high-fived, both wearing wide grins. "Come on." He waved me back out. Of course, I followed. We rode the waves for an hour before I got tired. I could tell that he could keep going, so I sat on my board, kicking lazy circles with my dangling legs while he caught two more.

When he paddled up to me, I laughed. I couldn't help it. It was exactly what I needed, and I told him so.

"I'm glad. It usually is for me too." He linked his hand with mine, and we bobbed on our boards for a few comfortable moments of silence. Without asking any questions, he seemed to have known that I was angry and hurt about what Charles had done. I appreciated the day more than he could've realized. It was, in a sense, cathartic. "Want to head in and grab something to eat at the Sandbar Grill?"

"That sounds great." I hadn't been hungry, but as soon as he mentioned it, I was ravenous. I dropped to my stomach on the board, and we headed to the shore. It didn't take too long. Even if it had, I didn't care. Everything was perfect, and I didn't want it to end. After stowing our boards by our stuff and spreading our towels for when we returned, we set off in the direction of the beachside restaurant.

By the time we got there, a line five people deep stretched from the window. There were two guys behind the couple at the front and a pretty blonde in an olive bikini who acknowledged Xander with a wave and "Aloha." She was tanned and toned and looked like she lived to surf. The guys turned around and stepped up to place their order, but the girl didn't move.

"When did you get back?"

The frown on her face snagged my curiosity. An old girlfriend? I waited for Xander's response.

"Not too long ago." He made introductions, explaining that her dad was the police chief who was recovering from heart surgery, the one his brother Jaxon was working for.

"Jackass is here?"

I froze, unsure what was going on or why she would insult his brother. It wasn't hard to figure out that her unflattering nickname was for Jaxon.

Xander winked at me. "Yep. I take it you haven't seen him? You staying with your dad?"

"I just got here."

"Bound to run into him, then."

"Kayla, put your order in." One of the guys tugged on her sun-kissed hair. With a troubled expression, she muttered a quick goodbye then stepped to the counter.

After they ordered, they moved away, and I let the encounter go. Xander had slipped his hand around my waist when he'd introduced me. I had nothing to worry about.

We placed our orders then took our food back to our towels. I sat and waited for him before eating. He popped the cooler and grabbed two bottled waters. He handed one to me then sat down, and we took the food out and dug in.

The sandwich crunched as I bit into it, and layers of cheese, bacon, lettuce, tomatoes, and a spicy sauce that I couldn't quite identify sang across my taste buds. Surfing was intense and calorie burning. Not to mention that I'd gotten up late and hadn't had time to eat. I washed my first bite down with water as Xander polished off half of his meat-lover's sandwich. It was called something else, but I couldn't remember the name. The gist of it was that it contained a heck of a lot of meat.

Conversation buzzed around us from the other people on the crowded beach. Thankfully, we had a small bubble of space with the surfboards.

"What got you interested in photography?"

His question startled me, and I jerked my gaze from the water. "I like to uncover the hidden layers of what I'm taking pictures of. Through the lens, things are revealed. I'm able to see more than I would without it."

"It lets you strip away preconceptions."

I laughed under my breath. "You nailed it. That's what it does."

"What are you looking to do with your grad degree? That's soon, isn't it?"

"Yeah, it's coming up fast. And I'll continue to do what I do. Two galleries in Chicago represent my work, but I may want to try for another in New York. Maybe not here, though." Living with my aunt hadn't been great, but she'd done something right for me and had invested my parents' life insurance money for me, which allowed me to do what I wanted. "If I decide to live here, I like anonymity. It makes life easier."

"I get that." Finished with his meal, he leaned back on his elbows and looked out over the water. "A little over a week isn't a lot of time to plan and secure where you want to go. You're renting, right? How long do you have on your lease?"

"Until June, so there isn't a huge rush after graduation in May. I'm not ready to make any rash decisions yet." I wanted to get off the topic.

"What about the ex? Does he figure into your plan?"

I finished chewing the last bit of my lunch and washed it down with a sip of water. It wasn't something I had to think hard about, but I appreciated his patience. There was no weird pressure or awkwardness with him. "Charles doesn't fit into my decision to stay or go. As far as I'm concerned, I won't have to deal with him after I graduate."

"He goes to the same college?"

Shoot. "You could say that." I didn't want to talk about me. I gathered our trash and put it in the carryout bag to throw away when we left. "You mentioned the island you're doing renovations on is family owned. Do your parents live here, too, and your two brothers?"

"We all do, except my parents are traveling. They're taking advantage of retirement, so we don't see them that much."

I mimicked his pose, leaning back on my elbow so that we

were lying on our sides but facing each other. "But you aren't normally around because of being in the military?"

"I'm not gone as often as you think. It's a few weeks out on missions here and there. Then we have time on base and also at home. I have no idea when I have to deploy next or when I'll be back. But it could be in two weeks."

I pointed to the circular scars that looked relatively recent on his chest. "Bullet wound?" It made sense. He seemed to be able to move around and even carry the boards with relative ease. I hadn't wanted to comment on them earlier, but it seemed like an appropriate time.

"Shrapnel." He frowned, and a shadow swept over his features. "I was lucky. It could have been a hell of a lot worse."

It was clear from the gruffness in his voice that Xander didn't want to go into any details. Or maybe he couldn't legally talk about it. I wasn't all that familiar with how the military worked. "What about your brothers? You mentioned you have two, right? Do you all plan to stay here, or have any of them moved away?"

He laughed, and I grinned back at him. That had been a lot of questions, but I wasn't embarrassed. I was genuinely curious.

"I'm the middle kid."

"Good to know. I've got a handle on your personality now," I teased.

He reached out and tugged on a strand of my dark hair. Mirth flashed in his eyes, and that sexy grin curving his lips kept distracting me too. I couldn't help but wonder if he was going to kiss me at some point. I blinked quickly, surprised by my train of thought so soon after I'd broken up with Charles. *Does this mean I didn't love him as much as I'd thought?*

"You may think you have a handle on my personality."

I jolted back to our conversation, grateful for the distraction from my thoughts. "Oh, I do. As the middle kid, you're trouble." I let my gaze linger on the wound then travel to a few other faint scars. "Maybe a thrill seeker too? With an older and a younger brother, you probably had to fight for attention, which caused you to act out. Maybe you're a little wild?" I raised my eyebrows.

"I guess you'll have to wait and see."

His voice dropped to a sexy purr, and I fought a full-body shiver. We were getting into dangerous territory. Part of me, the side that felt used and betrayed by what Charles had done, welcomed it. But even with Xander's flirting, he never made me feel like an object, unlike Charles, with his roaming eyes and inability to focus or care about what I had to say.

Again, my gaze strayed to Xander's lips. I couldn't fight against the pull he had over me. He picked up on the cue and leaned toward me, catching another stray lock of my dark hair and tucking it behind my ear. I shivered despite the heat. His fingers trailed lower then hooked behind my neck, pulling me closer. When we were an inch apart, he paused, giving me time to pull away. I didn't want to. I inhaled sharply. Then his lips brushed over mine, slowly and softly. With each pass, my head swirled, and our surroundings faded.

Need and desire consumed me, and any internal battle to slow things down went up in flames. When his tongue teased the seam of my mouth, I opened for him. He slanted his lips over mine, urgency guiding both of our reactions. Tingles spread from his touch, and I tangled my tongue with his. He applied gentle pressure on the back of my neck to draw me closer, and I flattened myself against him, moaning at the contact. With each ridge, dip, and swell of muscle, I had to fight the small amount of awareness I had not to squirm against him.

I'd never imagined a kiss like that in my wildest dreams—all-consuming, uninhibited, and passionate.

Pinpricks of sand hit our lower legs, followed by the giggle of children, and with reluctance, we parted. We both breathed heavily as the world filtered back in, and I hurried to put some distance between us. Desire swirled in his gaze, and I swayed closer, wanting to fall back into his more-than-capable embrace.

I pressed my fingers to my swollen lips, where I could still feel him, missing his touch already. And I made a decision. I could be alone like my aunt, or I could trust once more, risking my heart and possibly much more. Because I knew from that kiss that if I wasn't careful, I could lose myself in him.

10

RILEY

Work was a blur in more ways than one. I couldn't stop thinking about spending time with Xander at the beach the day before... or that kiss. It was a good thing I was done for the day and almost home.

I tripped going up the second-floor stairs. My arm shot out, gripping the railing to prevent an unfortunate face-plant. Laughing, I shook my head, grateful that no one witnessed that stellar moment. I jogged up the rest of the way, in too good a mood to let anything get to me.

If only I could have hung onto that feeling.

I rounded the corner and skidded to a stop. My gaze locked on my apartment door, and I froze. It was open. My heart thudded inside my chest, echoing in my ears. The first time the door had been shut, but not this time. It wasn't a coincidence. I refused to believe that.

Terror crawled over my skin like a thousand fire ants. With hands that shook, I pulled my cell phone from my pocket and pressed 9-1-1. When the operator came on the line, I told her what had happened, where I was, and that I didn't feel safe going in there. She told me to leave the building and wait for the officer outside. It would only be a matter of minutes, she said, as an officer a few blocks away was responding.

I flew down the stairs as if someone was on my heels. The entire way, I fought the urge to look over my shoulder. Tears streamed down my face, and I swiped them away then burst through the entrance doors. Air sawed in and out of my lungs, and once outside, I let myself look behind me. No one was there.

Time passed slowly, and I didn't ease my tight grip on my phone until the awaited police car rolled to a stop in front of me, the word "police" clear on the side. I took a half step forward then jolted to a standstill, unsure of what I should do. *Wait for them to come to me? Probably.* I shoved my phone into my pocket and clasped my hands tightly together to still the tremor.

The squad car door opened, and a uniformed officer got out then rounded the front of the vehicle and stood before me. I had enough sense to register how attractive he was but little else. Nothing mattered. I wanted—no, needed—to feel safe. On the heels of that thought came Xander and the urge to call him. Even after such a short time knowing him, I'd latched on to the ease with which he took charge and how safe I felt near him. But with the hot cop in front of me, I forced myself to release my hands from the tight fists I'd been making.

He flashed identification, and I caught something military on there in my hasty glance. It was odd, but in the moment, I didn't really care. I needed help.

"I'm Jaxon. Are you the one who called in the break-in?"

"Yes." I stuck my hand out to him, surprised by how much he looked like Xander. *Maybe this is his brother.* "Riley. I live on the third floor."

"Are you all right?"

I nodded. "Just nervous." Mentally, I shook my head at the way my thoughts were ping-ponging.

Jaxon smiled. "That's understandable." His lips curved into a smile that I was sure was meant to put me at ease. It didn't work, though. I was incredibly stressed, and I wasn't sure what waited for me when I entered my apartment.

"Let's go take a look." I let him know that the elevator was ancient, and instead, we climbed the stairs together in silence, which I preferred. I had to quicken my pace to match his longer legs. When we got to my door, which still stood ajar, he turned to me. "Wait here for a minute while I do a sweep inside to make sure no one is there."

I nodded and tucked myself against the wall by the side of my door. He didn't have to tell me twice. There was no way I would go in there. If someone was waiting... I shuddered at the thought of what could have happened.

A few minutes passed before he came out and gave me the all-clear and instructions not to touch anything. I walked the apartment with him by my side, checking to see whether anything was missing or stood out to me as significant.

When I came to my bedroom and found my clothes strewn about, slashed, I swayed on my feet. He grasped my elbow and assured me that it would be all right. A detective was on the way, along with a photographer.

Will it be okay? I hoped so. Again, Charles and his quick temper flashed briefly in my mind, but I kept it to myself. I was confident that he wouldn't have destroyed my clothes or anything else. It wasn't how he operated.

As it was Sunday and likely that the other residents could have seen something, the officer had one of his team go door-to-door and question them. The lock had been tampered with, and he roused the landlord to change it while he waited. It was good that Jaxon was there, but I also wanted everyone to leave so I could fall apart without witnesses. My growing feeling of vulnerability and the sense that something bad was coming were like monkeys on my back. Thankfully, my wine was intact.

I planned on having a large glass or maybe the whole bottle once they cleared out.

Soon after we entered, a team came in and processed the break-in. What felt like horrific days had only been hours. Jaxon motioned for me to move to the side of the room with him. I followed then leaned up against the wall.

"Do you mind if I ask you a few questions?"

"That's fine." I shoved my hands into the back pockets of my jeans, not knowing what to do with them.

"Were you home when the break-in occurred?"

What? "Um, no. I came home from work, and the door was open." I decided it was best to withhold that the door had been unlocked the other day. He was giving me a standoffish vibe, and I didn't want to deal with the same accusations that it was my fault that Charles had leveled.

"Did you go into your apartment when you first learned it was tampered with?" His dark eyes had intensified, and that same sense of security I felt with Xander washed over me, just without the instant attraction. They had to be related.

"No. I called 9-1-1, and the operator instructed me to wait for you outside."

"Does anyone live with you or have keys to your apartment?"

Thank God I never gave Charles a key. That was one thing I didn't need to worry about. "No. I live alone, and no one has access other than the landlord." I wanted to head off more of the questions. "I know I locked the door behind me when I left for work at five this morning. No windows were open or unlocked."

He nodded, and I was struck again by how much he reminded me of Xander. Not a bad thing at all.

"Did you notice anyone different in the building or driving away when you came outside?"

"No." I shifted then tightly clasped my hands once more to stop my nervous movements.

"Any salespeople or contractors in the last couple of days?"

"No."

"Is this the first time this has happened? And do you have any idea who may have broken in?"

Charles crossed my mind, but that would have been too weird. It wasn't something he was capable of. Nor did I want to draw attention to him and risk his career, no matter how upset with him I was on a personal level. Having the police question him, possibly on campus, wouldn't be a good scenario. "No." Besides, he would have been in class while I was working. I dismissed the passing thought. It wouldn't have been possible. I didn't want to lie, though. "It was open one other time, but nothing was missing or disturbed. It's possible that I forgot to lock the door."

Nothing appeared to be missing, but the crime felt very personal, and Jaxon was concerned, asking if there was someone I could stay with. Ava was married, and I didn't think she was a possibility as she traveled a lot, and I didn't want to be alone with her husband. I thought of Xander and the island, but I barely knew him. Instead, I convinced myself that I would be fine alone—*I hope.*

11

XANDER

I stood with Tyler just outside of the burger joint where we'd had lunch. We were both frustrated with how Daryl was running things. Our unit was tight, and the recent deaths and changes in leadership were taking a toll.

"Are you coming out to the island to give me a hand with the reno?" I didn't need the help, but I wanted to keep him close. I was worried about him—about all of us. The problems and ambushes we'd encountered made things feel unstable. I couldn't lose my brothers. My chest got tight any time I thought about how I'd had Kyle in a fireman's carry after he'd been hit hardest from the blast. When I'd first gotten him over my shoulder, he'd been alive—barely. By the time we'd made it back to the extraction point, he wasn't.

"Not until later. Besides, aren't you trying to get your girl there?" His grin widened, and he leaned against the brick wall of the restaurant.

Riley—yeah, I wanted her there with me. She invaded my thoughts all too often. She wasn't native to Hawaii, but she had similar hair, long and dark, hypnotizing whiskey-colored eyes, full, pouty lips, and a long, lean body with just the right curves. I always wanted her.

"Hey, isn't that Mark?" Ty turned his head as two guys left the mosque across the way.

"Looks like him." The guy he was with triggered my instincts, none of them good. He was close to the same height as Mark, with the same dark wavy hair and similar facial features. The difference was in the way he moved, the hardened gaze when he spotted us, and the way he pushed in toward Mark to mumble something that wouldn't carry.

Ty raised his hand and shouted across the street.

Mark noticed us then said goodbye to his friend, who turned and went back inside. Mark jogged across the street to us. "Did you eat there?" He indicated the restaurant behind us. "I love that place."

"Yeah, it's great." Ty sounded distracted, but his eyes were sharp. "Who was that guy you were talking to?"

"Nasir." Mark flashed a wide smile. "Turns out we're related. How crazy is that?"

"Very," Ty replied.

I let my brother pursue it without intervening. He usually had an angle and filed data away for when it was needed.

"I met him through Anna." Even when he shrugged, he couldn't diminish how obviously happy he was, how content. "I wanted to meet up with you, so this works out well. Anna hasn't noticed anything, but she's concerned about how things went in Colombia." A flash of pain briefly crossed his features before he masked it. "She and Kyle were close, so she's invested too."

"We'll get to the bottom of it." Ty went to punch his arm but pulled back at the last second, turning it into a light tap. "I've got to head out. Glad to see things are going well for you. Later, Mark."

We said our goodbyes, then Ty and I headed to my truck so I

could drop him back at base. We didn't speak until we were inside with the doors closed. "That was painful."

"No shit. Kyle was a major problem for Mark." Ty snapped his seat belt in place. "With both of them on the lookout for a money trail or any communications that'll help us figure this out, we should hear something."

I hoped so, and before it was too late.

———

Riley

BRUSHSTROKES OF DEEP RED, pink, and orange painted the sky and reflected across the shifting ocean as the sun's fiery orb sank below the horizon. The beauty soothed my troubled soul, the gentle breeze promised change, and the wine lulled me into a semblance of calm after the meltdown I'd had when the last officer left my apartment.

Through swollen, irritated eyes, I followed the path of a night heron as it dove at a sharp angle then broke the surface of the water, emerging with its prey in its mouth. I felt like that unlucky fish, waiting for the next unexpected attack, which I hoped with everything in me wouldn't come. But superstitions were hard to shake, and for me, things always happened in threes—sometimes double that.

There were only two weeks left of classes and then graduation. I took another sip of my cabernet, enjoying how its warm spice danced over my tongue. When life was so unstable, it was easier to appreciate the little things like a gorgeous sunset, a beautiful night, and good wine. I'd thought, with Charles, that I'd found that elusive security and partnership I'd craved since having to move in with my aunt all those years ago. I had been so wrong. I pursed my lips and glanced at the beach not far from my apartment as a couple walked hand in hand, the woman's musical laughter reaching my ears. I longed for what they appeared to have.

Chimes sounded from my phone, and I jolted as the noise pierced my semi-relaxed state, causing several drops of red to splash over my pink pajama pants. Scowling, I brushed at them, making the situation worse. Ignoring the stain for a minute, I set my wine on the end table and picked up my phone. I swiped at the answer button to accept the call after seeing that it was Ava.

I forced a lightness to my voice when I heard hers, as I desperately wanted to pretend everything was normal. She wasn't buying it, especially when an unwelcome tremor stole into my greeting.

"What happened?" Ava demanded.

When she used that tone, I knew there was no pretending everything was fine. She would hound me until I spilled the details. Resigned, I recounted what had happened that afternoon, down to the torn clothes and none of the neighbors seeing or hearing anything unusual.

"Are you all right?"

I pushed my hair back from my face, giving her question a little bit of thought. "Yes." I was shaken up, but I wasn't physically hurt.

"I can cut my trip short, come home early, and stay with you. I could be there by tomorrow morning."

My heart swelled at her offer. "Thank you, but I'll be fine." And I would be. Whatever was happening would not break me. That had happened a long time ago, and I'd picked up the pieces that were salvageable and was stronger for it.

She launched another inquisition to ensure I was indeed okay, and then we chatted for a few more minutes. It was good to hear her voice, and I laughed at the awkward situation she'd found herself in when the head of the convention center caught her geeking out in sweats with her hair a mess, reading her favorite book. It wasn't the professional image she tended to portray. I needed to get a copy of that book. She swore by the author, C. Marx, and if anything could ruffle Ava's immaculate appearance, I wanted to check it out too.

I was laughing at another story she shared when someone pounded on the door to my apartment.

"Are you expecting anyone?" Ava's sharp words added to my spiked anxiety.

"No," I whispered. "Maybe I should ignore them. They'll go away."

"I think you should answer it."

"What? Why?" I could hear her tapping a pen on a hard surface.

"I'll be listening with you, and if it's anyone threatening, I'll call the police immediately. Plus, they won't try anything while you're on the phone."

I wasn't so sure about that, but I got up and made my way to the door anyway. Even so, I wasn't going to open it without knowing who was there first. "Who's there?"

"It's me, Riley. Open up."

I rested my head against the door as both relief and aggravation washed over me. *What is Charles doing here?*

"Well?" Ava asked.

I'd forgotten she was on the phone. "It's Charles. I'll let you go, but thanks for being there for me, Aves."

"Pfff. As if I wouldn't be. And why are you letting him in? I thought you kicked him to the curb and were dating the hottie instead."

I grinned at her descriptions. "Yes to both, but I'm taking things slow. I'll find out what Charles wants then get rid of him." A small part of me was still suspicious, and I wanted to see his reaction in case he had been the one responsible for breaking in.

"Stay strong."

"Most definitely." I said goodbye and hung up before opening the door for Charles. I stepped back, and he walked in. I'd already picked up the mess, stuffed the slashed clothes into a garbage bag, and tossed it in the dumpster, where I wouldn't have to be reminded of them again.

I shut the door and crossed my arms. "What are you doing here?"

He pivoted and faced me, his appearance disheveled. There were bags under his eyes. He looked tired. "I came so we could talk about what's going on with you. So we can fix things."

Why won't he take no for an answer? Using the element of surprise, I asked the only question I cared about. "Did you break into my apartment?"

His head jerked back as if I'd slapped him. "This again? Why would I do that? And when would I have time to, if it was even in the realm of possibilities, which it isn't because that's idiotic." He shook his head. "This is so typic—"

"The police were here today." I cut him off, not willing to listen to his belittlement and condemnation. "A lot of my clothes were slashed."

He paled then pressed his lips together in a straight line so tight that they were leached of color. "I should stay the night. That would be safer for you."

As if. "Did you have anything to do with that?"

He waved away my question with his hand. "God no, and I'm surprised that you would even contemplate me having anything to do with something so petty, so plebian."

I rolled my eyes. It took all kinds to break the law, and if he would remove the privilege from his shoulders, he would understand that.

"I should look around."

"What do you think you'll find that the police didn't?"

Before I could stop him, he turned and walked through the living room and kitchen, passing the bathroom on the way to my bedroom. Then he backtracked when something obviously caught his eye. "Why is your bikini drying on the curtain rod?"

"Obviously, I went swimming, not that it's any of your business."

"When did you have time to do that?" He turned to me, the color swiftly returning to his face, and his nostrils flared. "Did you go with anyone?"

Nope. We aren't doing this. "Thank you for answering my questions. I'm tired. It's been a long day, and it's time for you to go."

"I'm not going anywhere," he said with a growl.

The hell he wasn't. "You know, I didn't tell the police about your temper when they asked me if anyone came to mind who might have broken in or destroyed my clothes. Your behavior is making me second-guess myself."

Charles huffed as he strode past me to the door. He paused, spearing me with a glance over his shoulder. "This isn't the end of us, Riley."

"You're married. It's over." My own anger flared at his veiled threat. "If you think to flunk me or affect my grade in any way out of spite, for a class which I will be finishing remotely, I will be forced to tell the police, the university's board, and your wife about us—in great detail. We are done. Stay away from me."

His lip curled into a sneer. Before he could say anything else, I slammed the door shut behind him then slid the bolt home and sagged against the solid wood. I needed to get a security chain installed. *Will this day ever end?*

1 2

R I L E Y

With a full cup of coffee in hand, I clicked send on the emails I'd addressed to each of my three professors. All assignments due were attached, and I requested that I handle the upcoming ones from home as well. I would go in for tests or to deliver my portfolio, which was almost complete. I still had some editing to do.

It was not the best way to start a Monday, but I wouldn't step foot on campus after the break-in and confrontation with Charles. I needed a mental breather.

The sound of my phone ringing pulled me away from my laptop, and I set it aside, making sure to see who was calling before answering. It was Melanie, and I frowned as I said hello.

"Hey, Riles. Can you cover my shift this afternoon?"

"I can't. I've got plans with a boatload of homework." That was partially true. My homework was slotted for the morning, and I was heading to the beach with Xander later, which I would not trade in for covering her shift.

A few seconds passed. "Is it homework or Charles?" Her voice vibrated with fury.

I didn't want to get into it with her. We'd been there and

done that. And I hoped she would get over him soon, because she'd been a good friend before. "No. I'm not dating Charles." My other line beeped, and I almost sighed with relief. "I've got to go. Another call's coming in." She started to say something, but I'd clicked over to Ava. I pushed aside the awkward and overly jealous call with Charles's apparent stalker and said hello to Aves, hoping the tension wasn't apparent in my voice.

"I thought I'd call and see if you were all right." Ava's voice sounded wary. "Or if the professor spent the night."

"What?" I paused with my cup lifted halfway to my mouth then shook my head, even though she couldn't see it. "No way. I kicked him to the curb for the last time."

She laughed. "Okay, good. I was worried." Silverware clinked against a glass, and I could picture her with a cup of freshly brewed coffee.

"You shouldn't be. I have no plans to take Charles back. Honestly, I can't believe I wasted six months on his lying ass." I shifted in my seat and clicked around on my laptop, bringing up the pictures that I would need to edit for my final portfolio then a few I planned to send to the gallery. Scrolling through, I found a few I'd snapped of Ava when we had gone shopping. I'd promised her that I would send them to her later that day.

"I'm still stunned that he's married."

"You and me both. It takes a special kind of douchebag to cheat on his wife."

"Hmm. How in the world did he keep the relationship with you secret?"

I grimaced. *Through my naïveté.* "It was probably easy for him at first. We only met at my place or his office."

"You never went out anywhere else with him? No restaurants, movies, nothing?"

"This is embarrassing." I abandoned sorting through my pictures and instead looked out the sliding doors to the lanai that offered a glimpse of the ocean. "After he wore me down and I agreed to go on a date with him, he would suggest things like a picnic in his office or remote restaurants. I did so because I wanted to protect his career. If he'd been seen with me, it could've been a problem."

"Wow, that's so romantic."

I could picture Ava's eye roll. "Right. It wasn't. And when he complained about never having home-cooked meals, I invited him to my apartment. That became our routine, with the occasional drive to a distant beach where we would spread out a blanket, sip wine, and talk." Among other things.

"Talk?"

"For a little while." I didn't want to admit how little we talked. "Honestly, he was incredible when we were first seeing each other. The way he treated me and the belief he had in me helped to build my confidence. He got me involved and out of my shell. He helped me see my strengths, something I wasn't used to looking at. And he's so smart. But there were a few negatives too." He wasn't interested in my photography, not really. Oh, he pretended at first, but I'd caught him with one too many glazed expressions to fool myself for long. I'd adjusted my expectations and instead let him monopolize our conversations with his concerns or accomplishments. I'd learned my lesson and wouldn't do that again.

Toward the end, I think he was tired of me. Not only did I suspect he was still seeing Melanie, but there may even have been someone else, despite his insistence in winning me back, which was possibly completely ego-driven.

My thoughts drifted to Xander and how different it was when we were together. He was attentive, listened, and asked questions. It wasn't a one-sided conversation, and I never felt like he was only thinking about how soon before he could get me into bed. He had an aura of confident control, but not in a way that would override my opinion.

"I'm not trying to be judgmental here, but you didn't think it was odd that he never took you out to the movies or even to walk around town?"

I rubbed my forehead and leaned back in my chair, suddenly exhausted. "I did, and when I brought it up to him, we argued. I had a lot on my plate, too, with work and school. Trust me. His unwillingness to do anything different was a point of contention between us. And the more I pushed him away, the more we fought."

"He sounds like a child deprived of a shiny new toy. I've warned my husband against cheating."

"I'm sure your husband is nothing like Charles." I felt terrible that I could have caused an issue with Ava's marriage by having her watch me go through this with a married man. I was sure it would manifest certain fears for most women.

Ava's sigh echoed my own weariness. "Are you sure you're okay?"

I thought about when he first approached me and how I should have looked at him through my camera's lens. For some reason, that revealed hidden layers I didn't normally pick up on. "I will be if he leaves me alone."

"You need to draft an email to the board about his conduct and have it ready in case he continues to harass you. Use it as a threat if he comes around again. All you would need to do is hold your phone up, your thumb hovering over send. A peek at the contents should be enough to make him back off if his career and reputation are threatened."

I sat up straight, pivoting toward my computer. "That's a great idea." I opened a new email and jotted a note in the body of it so I would remember what needed to be written when I got off the phone.

An email about a recent purchase landed in my inbox, and I welcomed the news as a change of topic. Charles had taken up entirely too much of my morning. "I ordered that book, *The*

Spider's Prey, that you were reading the other day. Since you and Mel like C. Marx's work so much, I wanted to check it out too."

"Oh, you'll definitely find it interesting. Let me know what you think."

I grinned, looking forward to its arrival. It would be a welcome distraction from my life.

13

RILEY

That afternoon, the sun beat down on Xander and me. I loosely wrapped my arms around my bent knees, digging my toes in the sand. Waves rolled in the distance, and the droplets of water that had beaded on my skin after our hour of surfing had long since dried. We'd stretched out on beach towels in companionable silence. I didn't work that day, but I was scheduled for Tuesday. When he'd called early Monday morning, I jumped at the chance to have a day at the beach—in public.

This time, we'd gone to a military beach. It was less crowded, but there were still people around. The differences between Xander and Charles were many, and I loved every one.

Movement caught my gaze as a shirtless guy jogged close to the water's edge. Sweat glistened on his chiseled body, momentarily distracting me. He curved inward, and a curvy woman met him halfway, threw her arms around him, kissed him, then jogged back to her towel.

I turned back to Xander and experienced the familiar jolt of attraction.

I wasn't the only one who'd noticed the guy. A fierce frown

told me that Xander must know him and maybe didn't have the best relationship with him. When Xander shifted his focus to me, I swore I saw jealousy in those stormy eyes of his. "Do you know him?"

"Yeah. That's Daryl. He's a SEAL too."

"Oh. I take it you're not on the best terms?"

Daryl stopped running when he arrived at the pretty blonde reclining on a towel.

"It's nothing." Xander seemed to dismiss his mood and shrugged.

I cast one more glance at the couple and wondered why they seemed to be a source of discontent to Xander.

He leaned over and plopped my sun hat on my head. "Your nose is getting red."

"Thanks." I turned toward him as he mimicked my posture and smiled. He seemed to have moved on from our brief exchange over the other people. Longing for my camera, I promised myself I would bring it next time we were together and take some pictures. My gaze lingered on the small pink scar near his shoulder.

"Want to tell me about it?" Xander asked.

I jolted at the deep cadence of his voice, and my hat shifted from the sudden movement. "What do you mean?"

He adjusted my hat, his gaze boring into me. "You've been distracted sitting here. And when I catch you off guard, I can tell you're anxious from how jumpy you are."

Busted. I didn't want to talk about Charles, but the break-in was still bothering me. "My apartment was broken into the other day, and I've been pretty stressed since it happened."

"Were you inside at the time?" His gaze raked over me, and the easygoing Xander I'd come to know transformed. In his place was an intense and lethal soldier. I shivered from the instant metamorphosis but was oddly comforted.

"No." I waved away his concern. "I came home from work

and found my door open. I called 9-1-1 and waited until the police arrived to go inside. He looked a lot like you. I think he was your brother."

"Jaxon was there?"

"Yeah."

"Then yeah, he's my older brother. I'm glad he checked out your place and made sure it was safe. Did he find anything?"

I knew the officer had looked familiar. "No. It's a bit of a mystery."

His gaze turned speculative. "Do you think it was your ex-boyfriend?"

I weighed my options, but when it came down to casting a shadow on Charles, I wasn't too worried. Xander wasn't the police. "To be honest, it crossed my mind. He hasn't taken our breakup well. I watched his reaction when I accused him of breaking in, and he was shocked. I don't think it was him."

"But you're worried about him? Could he be behind the hit you took on the street the other day?"

"No. He's not at all like that, just bossy and condescending. I warned him that if he comes around, I'll drop his name to the police as a possible suspect. There's another ace I have up my sleeve, too, that will ensure he leaves me alone."

"Do you want to share what that is?" Mischief played around the corners of his mouth as he grinned. "Need any help?"

I laughed. "I've got it under control, but thanks for your willingness to help." Of course, my stomach chose that moment to growl, and loudly. I'd had a banana for breakfast and a salad before we got together, but after surfing, I was hungry.

Xander's grin widened. "Want to go into town and grab something to eat at one of the cafes? We can sit outside and have sandwiches."

I relaxed. It was normal, going out and doing stuff together. I let my guard slip a little more. "Since my stomach seems to be eating itself, that's probably a good idea."

We packed up. Xander carried the boards and the cooler, and I had the beach bags. Thankfully, we were dry from sitting on the beach after surfing. I slipped on my cover-up and climbed into his truck while he secured everything in the back.

With no classes or work to worry about that day, I enjoyed every unencumbered minute of my time with him. When we were settled with seat belts on and the windows down, he pulled out into traffic. I twisted my hair into a messy bun on top of my head and leaned against the backrest. It didn't take long until we were downtown, and Xander parked on the street in front of a cute little café. It was seat yourself, so we chose a table in the far corner of the patio. A waiter appeared, handed us menus, and took our drink orders.

We read the selections in silence. Only a handful of minutes passed before the waiter returned, and Xander asked me if I was ready to order. I nodded then gave the waiter my selection of a buffalo chicken wrap. I sipped my tea as Xander told him what he wanted.

We chatted about my classes and how I only had around a week and a half left until graduation, and then our food arrived. He inhaled his burger then chuckled. "They make the best burgers here. I'll be going native on the island. There aren't any restaurants."

"Are the kitchens completed in any of the cottages? Or will you have to cook on a grill or over a bonfire?"

"Two of the houses are close to being done. The kitchens are finished, just some minor painting and updates left. It's the others that need a full gut and reno."

A few times after surfing or carrying the boards and cooler, I'd noticed him rotate and rub his shoulder. "Are you going to be able to manage the renovation work on the island with your injury?" I hoped we would have time to go out again before he left. The thought of not hanging out with him anymore didn't appeal. He was fast becoming a friend and possibly much more. Other than Ava and sometimes Chloe or Melanie, he was the only person I saw outside of work or class.

He reached over and tugged at a long strand of my dark hair that had come loose from my hasty bun. "I lost you for a second there." I grinned, refocusing on the present, and he shrugged. "I'm healed well enough to get the work done on the island."

I hadn't seen a shrapnel wound before and wasn't sure how I felt about how easily he seemed to accept it. "Can you talk about what happened? Were you on tour?" I worried my bottom lip between my teeth. "I don't even know what you do, exactly." *Or what the correct military terms are.*

"It happened on mission last month." He pointed to his shoulder. "I recovered after on base. Now, I'm off duty and on leave for a few weeks, but that'll end soon."

Alarm skated along my spine. "Will you be leaving on deployment again?" I didn't want to let go of the possibilities between us so soon.

"It's possible, but not for a couple of weeks." Shadows darkened his eyes. "Normally, I wouldn't have taken leave after recovery. I'm able to get back into the action, but we have a new team leader—the guy who was jogging on the beach—and he likes to do things differently."

His voice changed when he mentioned the new person, and I got the impression he wasn't too fond of him. By his shuttered expression, he didn't seem open to talking about it, so instead, we finished our meal, engaging in an easy conversation that didn't center on his career. The entire time, I wondered if the change in leadership would cause dissention between himself and his team. I knew all about uncomfortable work situations.

For example, Melanie and I were having trouble getting along recently, but we tried. At first, things had been good. We had getting an MFA in common and several classes together. The catalyst for the tension between us was the theory class she'd recommended I take, specifically with our advisor, Charles.

After we finished and the bill was paid, we returned to his truck, and he drove me back to my apartment. Shades of pink, red, and orange infused the sky. As the sun descended, the colors would deepen to a vibrancy that was breathtaking.

He shut the motor off and went around to open my door. Taking my beach bag from me, he locked his truck then threaded his fingers through mine. We walked hand in hand up the stairs to my apartment. The silence between us was thick with tension, and the hairs on my arms and neck rose in anticipation. *Will he come in? Do I want him to?* Everything about him drew me in.

We paused at my door, and my usual nervousness at that point was there, but for an entirely different reason. After he handed me my bag, I fished my keys out. My hand shook as I tried to insert it into the lock. When his hand covered mine, steadying it, a warm buzz infused my skin where we touched.

Once I had the door open, I turned to face him, and his hand cupped my cheek. Warm brown eyes met mine, swirling with emotion that made me gasp. His other hand went to my hip, drawing me closer. I inhaled sharply at the contact, flattening my hands on his shoulders, so tempted to pull him closer. But I wanted him to make the next move. I needed to see where it was going, because I knew I was already a goner.

His gaze dropped to my lips, and in slow increments, he closed the distance, brushing his lips back and forth over mine. My heart skipped a beat, and a whimper escaped. With a moan, he deepened the kiss, his tongue invading my mouth in a teasing caress. I wrapped my arms around his neck and leaned into him as every inch of my body hummed in awareness and need.

All my worries evaporated in the fiery, passionate way he manipulated my mouth. I was completely unprepared by how the taste of him awakened uncontrollable desire.

He pulled me tight against him, and I sank into him, feeling how much I affected him too.

"Riley," he whispered before slanting his head and devouring my lips again.

Heat curled within me, and my knees went weak. The spark of love I'd felt bloomed, and I knew he could be the one.

After a few minutes, he drew back, resting his forehead against mine, our labored breaths mingling.

When he pulled back, his gaze was soft and tender, warring with the swirls of desire. "I really want to go inside your place, but I wouldn't be able to stop."

His husky voice vibrated from his chest into mine, and I almost purred, rubbing against him. But I forced myself to listen.

"There's something between us, Riley."

"I think so too." If he hadn't been holding me up, I would have swayed into him.

"I want to explore what's developing between us, and once you're ready, I want hours to savor you." Desire swirled in his gaze before his warm breath feathered across my face. Then he added more pressure and deepened the brief goodnight kiss.

Once inside my apartment, I leaned against the door, instantly missing the warmth of his body. My fingers pressed to my swollen, tingling lips. It had taken everything in me not to beg him to stay.

I meandered through my apartment, dropping my beach bag by my flip-flops then retrieving my damp towel and taking it to the washing machine. With my mind occupied by Xander, I peeled my off bikini and added it and detergent to the load.

Salty remnants from the beach clung to my hair and skin, and I got the shower going, checked the temperature, then stepped under the rainwater spout.

In a daze, I rinsed away the sand and salt but not the kiss. I couldn't help but wonder if Xander was already at his condo and in the shower too. My skin heated at the thought. After finishing up, I towel dried my hair, ran a brush through it, and slipped on pajamas.

It wasn't long until I had a glass of cabernet in hand and was settled on the veranda to take in the fading sunset. Exhaustion from the long day lulled me into a happy daze. Minutes passed in slow, delicious relaxation. When I finished my drink, I rinsed the glass then dragged myself to my bedroom. I slipped beneath my bedsheets with Xander's touch filling my mind, and I smiled, knowing I would have excellent dreams.

14

RILEY

Tuesday morning, the computer screen blurred for a moment, and I swiped my hand over my tired, gritty eyes. I needed a break. I stepped away from the pictures I was editing, poured another cup of coffee, added caramel-latte creamer, then went out onto the lanai to get away from my laptop.

Lunch was nearing, and after working an early shift at the Coffee Hut, I'd planned on spending the rest of the day and part of the next finishing up the projects that were coming due, at least as much as I could, so that I could skip classes and not worry about anything until graduation. I would only miss a handful of days, as class wasn't every day, and it shouldn't have been a problem. Then there was the upcoming weekend and one full week before graduation. I'd already spoken with two of my professors and gotten approval. It was the third who worried me.

The risk of running into Charles on campus was high, and I wasn't up for it. I kept a close eye on my grades in that class, too, just in case. Regardless of how I felt, I would have to go in two days before graduation to take a theory final. My grade was an

A, and I wasn't willing to chance it by skipping the exam. My gut tensed. I opened an email and shot off a request to the teacher's assistant for Charles's class, asking if he could administer the test. I included times when I knew he wouldn't be available and blamed it on work. With that sent, I forced myself to stop worrying about him.

It was a hot day, and I wished I was at the beach, hanging out with Xander, instead of cooped up in my apartment, trying to get my schoolwork finished. Tapping my foot, I nibbled on a fingernail and attempted to take a few minutes to myself before I went back in. It wasn't happening. I pushed out an aggravated breath and retrieved my laptop. The atmosphere was better outside, anyway, and the picture I'd been playing with nagged at me.

I tapped the file and brought up one of Ava's portraits. I'd taken several. She wore a formfitting short-sleeved black shirt with a high neckline. Her blond hair was secured in her signature tight bun, and small diamond studs adorned her ears.

In the first picture, her body was turned away, and she looked at the camera over her shoulder with a slight tilt to her head. In the second, her body was angled away while she looked directly at the lens. In the third, I'd caught her with lips slightly parted, her head tilted a tad to the right, and a few soft tendrils of hair framing her face. That'd been a compromise, as I'd wanted her hair down for that shot. Getting her to do any other poses wasn't possible, as she'd declined the more artistic ones I'd wanted to try. The light and position of her body created an approachable and soft effect.

I hadn't seen her writing in the Coffee Hut that morning, and when I'd texted on a break, she responded immediately, saying she was on a tight deadline and adding that she needed complete quiet. She was working from home but would be free Friday. We set up a lunch date, and I couldn't wait.

My gaze strayed to her portrait once more. The headshots

were beautiful, but they made me uneasy. I couldn't manipulate them to portray what I wanted. Groaning, I palmed my cell and sent a text to Ava: *pictures done—want them emailed or show you on Friday?*

The three dots appeared, and I waited for her response. It came in one word. *Friday.* Nothing followed. She must have been swamped. I shrugged because I was too. Editing her pictures was how I procrastinated with assignments I had to finish for school. Closing her folder, I instead opened up the double-exposure-themed portfolio that was a portion of my graduate project. There wasn't much left, but I wanted to go over every picture and ensure it was my best work.

Along with the images, there were notes for each compiled in a document that would be submitted in conjunction with the collection. I loved working on themes and had learned quite a few new techniques in the graduate program. It had been well worth the move and investment.

Toggling through the twelve frames, I paused on an image of a woman I'd captured from a side view, with her toes digging into the sand, gazing out at the ocean. That was the one that I'd chosen to have a greater density. Her long hair fell in waves down her back. Shoulders bare, her arms were loosely clasped around her legs. The double-exposure image contained a faded, surreal one where she maintained the same position, but with her head thrown back, conveying a deeper meaning as she consulted the sky overhead. The conflicting posture accented whimsy with a dash of indecision to her emotions.

Many others showed glimpses at contrast or alignment with the nature around the person, hinting at synergy and symbolism. Each one told a story, conveying the emotions I'd caught. I loved them all and sought permission in the form of a model release so that I could sell them after leaving a copy with the university. That way, the project would be on file in the library.

There were two left to edit, along with notes to compile, and the portfolio would be done. Mostly. I was toying with more themes. I wanted to give the collection my all, and it didn't feel complete yet.

I played around with one of the two pictures, adjusting the contrast until I was satisfied with the results. The notes wouldn't take as long, and I planned to do them and the last touch-ups after I got something to eat. I set my laptop on the table then went into the kitchen, mixed a salad, poured a glass of tea, and sat at the small peninsula.

After rinsing my dishes and stacking them in the dishwasher, I returned to the lanai and my homework. I'd gotten situated and settled in with my laptop when several texts pinged from my phone. Had to be Ava. I grabbed it and swiped the screen to read them, and my stomach dropped. In a quick switch, I set my computer on the table before it slid off my legs and went inside to pour some wine before I reread the messages. With alcohol to fortify my resolve, I returned outside with both the full glass and the rest of the bottle. I had a feeling I would need it.

The string of texts was from Charles.

Who was the guy you were with at the beach? How long have you been seeing him? End it. I'll be over tonight.

His frustration and anger were palpable through the words, some of them in caps. My hands shook as I replied that he was ridiculous and to stay away because he wasn't welcome anymore. Before he could respond, I blocked him. Nervously, I bit my fingernail, contemplating what to do.

He didn't have a key.

I would be okay.

Either way, I typed in 9-1-1 and left it on the screen so that help would be on the way with a simple touch of the call button. I hoped that precaution would be enough.

———

Late that night, a knock sounded at my door. I knew that impatient two-knuckle rap. I stood in my pajamas with my palm resting against the bolt, unwilling to open it.

"Riley, it's Charles."

The remorseful tone to his voice told me I wouldn't need to call for reinforcements. I responded by telling him to go away. He wouldn't. Instead, he begged me to hear him out. I wouldn't open my apartment door. I slid down and leaned my forehead against the cool wood as he unburdened his soul. The only concession I would give him was listening.

"I told her."

His wife. My heart slammed painfully against my ribs at his confession.

"I got a lawyer and filed for divorce. We sat on the couch in the living room and talked. I can't stop thinking about you, Riley. You're the one I want to spend the rest of my life with, not her. You don't know what it's like, living with her. I'm not happy and haven't been in a long time."

I didn't ask what she'd said or if she was unhappy too. I drew my knees to my chest and wrapped my arms around them. *This isn't what I wanted.*

"Are you still there?" His voice was hoarse with emotion.

"I am." I closed my eyes against the futility of his plight and my unknowing hand in destroying his marriage and shattering another woman's world.

"I haven't been myself and took my frustrations about my situation out on you. It wasn't your fault. It wasn't fair. You had no idea what I was dealing with. I won't make that mistake again." He cleared his throat. "Come back to me."

"I can't," I whispered, unsure if he would hear me through the thick barrier of the door between us.

"Graduation is right around the corner. There won't be anything stopping us," he pleaded. "The divorce... she said she wouldn't contest it, if that's what you're worried about. Please,

Riley. We're good together." There was a wealth of pain and desperation in his voice.

Tears ran unchecked down my cheeks. "No, Charles." He would keep pressing me. I had to get through to him. "Our relationship was built on a lie. There isn't any trust. I would always question why you were late or if there was someone else. It will not work, nor am I willing to try." *And somewhere along the way, I fell out of love with you.*

"I need you."

"I'm sorry." I pushed away from the door, farther from where he sat on the other side. "Please go."

———

Xander

I KICKED my feet up on the ottoman as Jaxon came out to the porch and passed me a cold beer before he took the seat next to me. He had a sweet place on the beach in Honolulu, even if the condo was only a studio. My mind raced, and he shot me a knowing look.

"What's going on in that head of yours?" Jaxon asked in his usual smooth drawl.

"Have you found out who broke into Riley's apartment yet?" I hated that she was there alone. Whoever it was could come back, and I wasn't there to protect her. After she told me about the break-in and that Jaxon was the responding officer, I reached out to him immediately.

"No, nothing. In fact, there weren't any fingerprints on the clothes that were destroyed other than hers. I have to tell you, it looks a tad suspect."

Anger ripped through me. "That's bullshit. I told you about the other day how she was attacked on the street."

"But you didn't see it happen. I even double-checked for you, and there were no security cameras pointed in her direction."

"I saw the mark. She was gasping for breath." I clenched my teeth. "It wasn't fake."

Jaxon rubbed a hand over his forehead. "I didn't get that impression from her either. She was genuinely frightened. I'll do more drive-bys on her place when you're on the island." He let out a weary sigh. "There's a detective on my ass about this case. He thinks I'm gunning for his job, so he's making mine difficult."

I relaxed my jaw as understanding about his predicament filtered in. He'd probably poked his nose into the guy's work, finding holes and pressuring for alternatives on the case because Riley was important to me. Also, Jaxon was thorough at anything he did, and he likely didn't agree with whoever the detective was.

"I'll keep tabs on things." As the seconds passed, the tension eased. "What else is on your mind?"

I tipped the bottle to my lips then took a long pull, debating my answer. Silence hung between us as he waited. I'd looked at the mission from so many different angles. Talking to my brother could shed new light on what went wrong or reinforce what I worried about most.

"No matter how much I try to put what happened out of my mind, I can't shake the last mission."

"It was a shit show, all right," Jaxon agreed. "Eerily similar to the one I was on before. Losing John was huge, and how it happened…"

John had been my team leader too. It was a major blow when he was killed on Jaxon's last mission. And then there were Jaxon's injuries, which had concerned all of us. It shouldn't have gone down like that. Something had to change, and I worried that the something was Daryl, our new team leader. "Yeah, and that's just it. Why are we getting ambushed? Is it faulty intel or something worse?"

His penetrating gaze shot to mine. "A mole?"

Even him verbalizing that felt like a bad omen, as if uttering the possibility would make it a reality. "Could be." I scrubbed my hands over my face, wishing there was no problem.

"Have you talked to Mark again?"

"Yeah, and that's a good idea. But there's more." There was one other thing I wanted to share with him, as he hadn't served under Daryl, but he knew him. "I can't shake the problems we're having with Daryl." I'd learned he coveted a leadership position with Team 9, but then John died, and he got it. And then there was the last-minute op change that had resulted in Kyle losing his life.

"He's not John." Jaxon took a long pull from his beer. "It could take a while to acclimate to his ways."

I shook my head. "It's more than that." Jaxon had a point, though, and my suspicion about him could have been unfounded, colored by the personal distrust about how he'd stolen my girlfriend.

"Then involve Mark."

I nodded. It was a good plan, one I would talk to Ty about. In the meantime, I would go over the imaging from the last mission with a fine-toothed comb. One way or another, I would find out what went wrong and who was to blame.

15

RILEY

The early-morning sun warmed my shoulders as I walked through the soft sand on the secluded beach. It was in the mid-seventies, and puffy clouds dotted the sky, perfectly cutting the glare for the pictures I wanted to take. My white cotton sundress with spaghetti straps stirred in the breeze.

Today would be all about editing and work on my final graduate project. Tomorrow, I planned to spend part of the day with Xander. He'd texted me late last night, asking if I wanted to go to lunch before my shift. He would be heading to the island either that day or the next and wanted to see me before he left. I couldn't help the way my heart had raced. I'd said yes on the spot.

Not far from the water, I set my backpack down and pulled the tripod out. Once the legs were extended and secure in the sand, I locked my camera into position on top. I had a Bluetooth remote that I would hide in my hands to take the pictures.

After checking through the lens's view to make sure I would be in the frame when I moved to the front, I made the adjustments to the camera. The series would be double exposure.

After playing around with a few others, there were still several poses I wanted. I got into position to begin.

My phone pinged from the pocket in my backpack, but I ignored it. Blocking out the consecutive beeps, I focused on what I'd come to accomplish. There was limited time with the perfect light, and I wanted to get all of the shots within the same hour.

The first was a series of profiles: my back to the lens, hair in a loose braid, looking behind me, and chin to my shoulder, and then facing the camera with a final shot in the same position but with my head bowed.

Excitement pinged in my stomach as I checked the frames to make sure they were what I wanted. They were. I couldn't wait to get back and start editing, but I had to finish the rest. I did a series of fast-frame shots while spinning on the sand, arms out, carefree. The last required the camera close to the water. After setting it up, I held the hem of my dress and waded into the mostly still water. After several poses, I called it good.

Packing up didn't take long. The breeze picked up, and I smiled at the way the palm trees rustled overhead. The puffy white clouds were ushered out by several darker ones, and the salty air carried floral notes, charged with the increasing electricity. A storm had been forecast for today, which was one of the reasons I wanted to get the shots done closest to dawn. Thankfully, I got what I wanted accomplished—I couldn't risk losing time on this project.

It was so peaceful on the beach that I decided to hang out and relax for a little while, or at least until the grocery store was open. I figured I could beat the rain before I got back home.

Luck was on my side, and with grocery bags in hand, I walked back to my apartment while people hurried down the street and sidewalk to begin their day. With a hard yank, I pulled the apartment building's door open then trudged up the stairs. Wary from the recent trouble I'd been having, I slowed my steps and checked along the floor to make sure no one was there who shouldn't be. The neighbors on my floor mostly worked during the day, with the only stay-at-home mom at the end of the hall with her three-year-old son, and they were frequently out of the house at parks or doing other activities. It was close to eleven, so I doubted anyone on my floor would be home.

When it was clear there wasn't anyone around, I neared my door. Keys in hand, I grasped the doorknob then sagged with relief after there was no give when I pushed. It was locked. My fingers were shaking so much that it took three tries for me to get the key in, and once inside, I immediately slid the dead bolt home.

Moments later, I'd put the groceries away, made some tea, and opened the balcony door to let in a breeze until the rain came. I connected my camera to my laptop, downloaded the photos, then got to work.

I imagined the series as a window into the psyche. The portraits were where I wanted to begin. First, I switched the shot from color to black and white. The first solid image was with my back to the lens, my shoulder blades prominent and my head bowed. When I was satisfied with the lighting and adjustments, I layered in the photo of me facing the camera with a slight downward tilt to my chin, which made it look as though I was intensely peering at the camera. Then I faded the layer enough to give the impression I wanted.

Pain and defensiveness bled from the solid image, while the shadowy one promised retribution. I loved it. In a way, it was how I saw myself being once I conquered the fear. I was getting there. The move to Hawaii was a big part of that—cutting ties with the past and starting fresh felt good.

The rest of the pictures would be in a similar layout, but the psychological meanings would differ from playful to struggling to deceptive. I selected a side portrait with my head tipped back, eyes closed, and lips parted, changed the background to gray scale, and deleted my form, leaving only the outline of my head. Then I filled the inside portion of my head with a color picture of water that rose from the bottom half and stopped at the center of my open mouth. The image gave insight into what couldn't be seen and how the person was drowning, although it was only visible on the inside.

There were two more frames to finish, but my aching shoulders and back needed a break. Thunder rumbled outside. I picked up my tea and went to heat it before sitting out on the veranda to watch the storm roll in, one of my favorite things to do.

My phone pinged again. I walked by it, refusing to get derailed. The day was all about homework. There wasn't much time until graduation, and I had to turn my final assignments in early so I didn't need to go in for the classes. I wouldn't risk seeing Charles.

Just the thought of him soured my mood. How did we go so wrong? Once my photo project was turned in and I took the final for Charles's class, which I was glad would be administered by his teacher's assistant, I was strongly contemplating moving. Part of me didn't want to—I truly liked being around Xander, and then there was Ava and the fast friendship we had.

It was time to go. The recent problems and how things had changed for the worse with Charles pushed me further into the idea. I feared I was more like my mom and aunt—unlucky in love—than I'd thought. In the end, my aunt had had no one and hadn't been found for weeks after she'd died, and my mom had been married to a mean drunk who treated her with no respect. I didn't want either outcome. But if I was unlucky like they'd been, things would end badly, and I wanted to leave before events had the chance to escalate further.

The sky had grown dark and angry. Lightning split the horizon, and I waited, counting until the thunder rumbled. So long as the wind didn't change, I could remain on the veranda, watch the weather, and be a part of nature's outrage, which matched my general sense of unrest.

The next day, I would give notice at the Coffee Hut. I hadn't needed to work there, but it kept me occupied, and I enjoyed the interaction it'd provided. Otherwise, I was behind my camera or editing when I wasn't in class. But then Charles had happened. And my world changed all over again. I'd liked it for a while. Not anymore.

The problems with him worked against the other progress I'd made. I'd done so much hard work in counseling to banish the nightmare of my childhood, but the recent break-in, and his possessive behavior threatened to undo everything. I couldn't let history repeat itself.

16

RILEY

Xander's large hand clasped mine as we walked to the Coffee Hut. In a slow caress, his thumb moved over the back of my hand, causing my pulse to flutter. He'd picked me up and we'd gone to lunch. It was Thursday's highlight so far and what got me through the stress of last night.

Out of the corner of my eye, I took him in. Towering over me, his muscular body and arresting features drew every person's eyes as we passed. But it wasn't only that. He had a commanding presence blended with an easygoing vibe. Hard to describe, but it was an intoxicating mix.

In an hour or so, he would leave for his island to get to work on the cabins, but he'd made time to see me before he left. It meant something. Warmth spread through my chest over the effort he'd made.

"I wish you didn't have to work today. We could head up the coast and take in a live show at one of the resorts."

I shivered from the effects his deep baritone had on me. "Mmm, that would have been fun." I wasn't ready to tell him I planned to turn in my notice. It was time. As for moving away from Honolulu, I was almost positive it was the right thing to do, but because of him, I was also on the fence.

Things had been going well with Xander and me. The only dark spot was the anger and hurt I continued to harbor about Charles's persistent behavior. But all that was done—I hoped.

I should have been heartbroken, but I wasn't, not even a little bit. I chalked it up to how much we'd been fighting and the fact that he'd lied and hidden his marriage from me. It'd all added up to me pulling away.

The sign for the Coffee Hut swung perpendicular to the building, and Xander and I stopped before it in front of the large picture window. He gave my hand a tug, urging me to turn and face him. Our gazes met. I sucked in a stuttered breath, completely drawn to him. I inched closer.

He raised his hand and cupped my cheek, and all thoughts scattered. He was intense, barely contained energy. And when he was focused on me, I felt everything. His fingers shifted and threaded through the hair at the base of my head, and my lips parted. I wanted him to kiss me. I didn't care that we were in front of where I worked.

In slow increments, he lowered his head, giving me plenty of time to back away should I want to. Everything in me stilled. I didn't want to pull away.

His lips brushed mine in a teasing caress. My stomach clenched, and desire shot through me like whiplash. A moan slipped past my lips as he deepened the kiss and made my head swim. The world faded away—it was only the two of us. My arms looped around his neck. I pressed myself against his solid chest.

When he broke our kiss and pulled back, I couldn't make myself let go. I could've kissed him for hours.

I was grateful that his arms held me up, because I was shaky from the kiss. There was so much promise in it. *When will the next time be?* I already craved more. I wanted to explore all of him, completely guilt-free. And honestly, after several kisses with Xander, I was more than ready to take things further.

Maybe I would give Honolulu another shot if it meant I could continue to see Xander. My finger twitched, and I longed for my camera to capture those chiseled features that only enhanced the sensual curve of his full lips and telling dilated eyes. And... a picture of him would give me that window I needed to see him clearly, mainly because I didn't trust my judgment after so many mistakes before.

"Come to the island with me this weekend." His deep voice was hoarse with desire.

I nodded, dazed from the sensation of his arms around my waist, my lips swollen from his kiss. "Okay." The bells above the door jingled as a customer left, reminding me that I needed to get inside for my shift.

He grinned. "I'll pick you up at the harbor early Saturday morning."

I agreed, and he made me promise to be careful in the meantime. We settled on a time, and I vowed that I would bring my camera to capture his image. It was in my bag right now, but I'd forgotten it because I'd been so caught up in our date. The days would drag until I saw him next. Xander occupied my mind, and I looked forward to spending more time with him. He made me happy.

When I stepped inside the coffee shop, the chilled air cut through the humidity that attempted to follow me. Several strands of my long hair clung to my neck and back, the sticky air causing it to thicken much more than usual with curls and waves. I twisted it onto the top of my head, threading the end through a section of the bun to secure it. With the heavy mass off my neck, I felt better.

I waved to regulars and exchanged alohas, in a great mood and already eager for the end of my shift. Melanie rushed in behind me. Her harried expression let me know that her mood didn't match mine. When she dumped her purse in the back and sidled up next to me, her scowl turned into a sneer.

"Were you out with Charles again?" she practically growled.

We'd had that argument before. I wished Melanie had never overheard Ava's comment about me dating an advisor. "No. I'm not dating him."

Jealousy came off her in waves.

"And you shouldn't be, either. He's married."

A customer entered, and she got in one last shot. "I'm the one that told you about his class. If I had known what a slut you were, I never would have."

Holy crap. My mouth hung open. She'd never been that vicious before. And to be honest, I had no idea if Charles had been dating both of us at the same time, but from how she was lashing out, I suspected he might have been.

Wait a minute. She hadn't seemed surprised about Charles still being married. *Had she known?*

Jeffrey, our manager, came out from the back office and did some inventory, eliminating the chance for Melanie to attack me again. I kept busy and stayed out of her way. For the most part, she and I got along. But after that one comment from Ava about my advisor, she'd guessed who I was dating, and I became her enemy. At least Jeffrey and Chloe were nice. Chloe and I had grabbed lunch or a movie now and then. I had no hopes of repairing my friendship with Melanie.

Before Jeffrey headed to the back room again, I asked if he had a few minutes to talk. Melanie shot daggers at me, probably because she thought I would tell on her, but I wasn't going to. It wasn't worth it, and I could fight my own battles when it came to her.

I followed Jeffrey into the back room that served as both office and stockroom. The shelves were packed with coffee beans and the mixes that didn't require refrigeration. Jeffrey maneuvered his lanky frame into his desk chair and waited for me to get to the point.

My bag was in one of the cubbies set aside for employees. I withdrew my resignation letter and handed it to him. I'd sent an email that morning but knew he wouldn't get to those until the afternoon.

"I'm giving my two-weeks' notice. And I wanted to thank you for everything you've done for me. Working here has been a lot of fun."

He placed the paper on the corner of his desk. "I wish you weren't going, but I understand. As for the two weeks"—he waved to a stack of applications—"that's totally up to you. I know you're nearing the end of grad school, and it's a hectic time. I can fill your spot whenever you're ready."

"Thanks." I would miss how easygoing he was. "I think I'll take you up on that." I would keep my last scheduled shifts. I promised to stay in touch, and I would. He and Chloe were good friends.

My four-hour shift flew by, and before I knew it, I was stepping outside and fiddling with my camera to get the nature pictures I wanted to incorporate into my project. It was the last theme I would add. It had to be, as I needed to turn the collection in before the weekend.

It was the perfect day for what I had planned. The rain had come while I was inside, and while a majority of the clouds remained, the downpour had slowed to a light mist. Even that was clearing, and I knew I could find some beautiful shots.

The university wasn't far, and I headed that way. There were several stunning gardens that I wanted to take a few close-ups of, and I could get home easily from there.

Not only did I plan to take pictures of the sweet, fragrant plumeria blossoms there, but I had also asked Chloe to pose for me with a velvety flower over an ear. If worn on the right, the wearer indicated she was single. I toyed with the idea of having

Jeffrey switch the flower on Chloe—it would be a romantic shot and could get her to see him as more than her boss. He was on the shyer side, though, and I doubted he would ask her out unless she gave him some sort of sign.

Later, I would cast a plumeria lei in the water and photograph it before dusk. I wanted to freeze the beauty of the flowers with an atmosphere of uncertainty. Long ago, when ships sailed, a lei was set adrift in the water. If it returned to shore, the vessel would too. If not, all those lives would be lost in the ocean.

Plumeria petals tossed into the water were meant to honor the fallen. The flower was chock-full of meaning, the perfect vehicle for the final series in my graduation project. Once the editing was done, the collection would be too. I couldn't wait to turn it in. Not only that, but the galleries would also love them. I planned to use all the pictures to seek representation at a high-end New York gallery, expanding my exposure and reach.

The sound of a car door pierced my consciousness but didn't fully yank me from the trancelike state I was in while snapping pictures of the flowers. I blinked as a shadow fell across the lens, and I lowered my camera. Pinpricks of alarm shot from my hands, up my arms, and into my head. The tight and uncomfortable sensation from the loss of concentration amplified the shock and fright I felt when I saw Charles standing before me.

I took an involuntary step back. My camera slipped from my fingers. The strap at my neck pulled taut from the weight of the camera hanging from it. I took another step to the side. He mirrored my move. We played a game of it while I tried to put distance between us, but he wouldn't let me.

His thick hair was mussed, as if he'd run his fingers through it. Lines bracketed his eyes and mouth. It looked as if he'd lost sleep. A second passed, then another. I could acknowledge how charming and handsome he was and why it had been so easy to fall for him. But I couldn't let those things or how things had been when they were good sway me. He was a classic example of my past, of what I had to fight against. My dad had been charming too. I wouldn't fall into the same pattern as Mom had. The end result would cost more than I was willing to pay.

"Riley, please." Charles extended his hand, a mix of frustration and sadness clouding his eyes. "I miss you. This whole thing has been a big mistake. Give me a chance to explain."

Explain what? His wife? Maybe the break-ins? What explanation could he possibly give to make me forgive him? With a sharp shake of my head, I forced my response between clenched teeth. "There is no explaining away a wife."

Anger chased the contrite expression from his features. My fingers curled around the phone in my pocket. I yanked it out and spared a second to look at the screen. With a few taps, I had the drafted email to the board visible. My thumb hovered over the send button, and I turned it toward him so he could see.

"Leave me alone, or I'll hit send."

His eyes darkened with anger when I issued my threat, my promise to impact his career if he continued to harass me.

He took a step back. "I've altered my life so that we could be together and made sacrifices you have no idea about." As he pivoted to retrace his steps, he issued a final promise. "This isn't over, Riley."

My entire body was rigid. It was over for me, and I suspected the same for him. That last comment had to be to save face—I couldn't see him risking his career. It took several seconds until I was able to move my thumb away from the send button and leave for home.

17

RILEY

I shifted in bed late Thursday night with the sheet tangled around my legs, and the cool breeze from the overhead fan couldn't keep the nightmares at bay. Sinking further into the memory of my past, the slow paddle above me from the fan faded, replaced by Mom's frantic eyes and quivering voice. As she invaded my sleep-laden mind, I was suddenly seven years old again and experiencing the catalyst for my recurring nightmare.

At the kitchen table, I chewed my peanut-butter-and-strawberry-jelly sandwich as quietly as possible. They were arguing about "never wanting this," whatever that meant. Dad's voice boomed from the next room so loudly that I looked over my shoulder to make sure he wasn't standing behind me. A shiver racked through me, causing my arm to bump the plate.

The shouting stopped. Mom rushed in. She bent over me. Her fingers bit into my shoulders, and I clamped my teeth on my lower lip to keep from making any noise. With my eyes as wide as they would go, I peered around her to make sure Dad was in the other room. He was. I felt sick. Those lines around

Mom's mouth made me uneasy, as did Dad's loud voice when he yelled for her.

"I want you to go out and play, sweetie. Okay?"

Her voice sounded weird, so I nodded. I didn't want to go outside. It was cold. But saying no would get me in trouble. I let her help me get dressed.

A hat was shoved onto my head, and she settled my coat around my shoulders, hastily zipped it, then hurried me to the back door. My boots were there, and she bent to help me put them on. We didn't say anything. Fear kept my lips pinched. I didn't want to make a sound. If I did, he would come into the kitchen. When he was mad, he was scary—not like when we watched princess movies together. I liked those times best.

Mom squeezed me tightly then released me and opened the back door. "Go on, sweetie. To the swings, baby girl." She glanced behind her then turned wide eyes back to me. "Only come in for me. I'll call you in later, m'kay?"

I stepped out into the chilly air, grass crunching beneath my boots. The door shut, and I looked over my shoulder, hoping to see Mom in the window, but she was gone.

I didn't go far, not right away. We had an old brown swing set that was wasn't like the one at the playground. Ours creaked and only had two swings. I had to wear my mittens to hold onto the chains without getting scratched.

The shouting inside grew louder. Dad yelled for me to get into the house. My steps halted, and I held my breath. A loud crash sounded like when I accidentally dropped a glass once.

I didn't know why Dad was so mad. He got that way sometimes. But this time, all the hair on my arms and neck stood up like it did when there was a bad storm. I didn't like it or know what to do.

Shuffling my feet, I kicked at a frozen tuft of grass for a little while. When the sounds inside didn't get quieter, I moved toward the swings. Tears rolled down my cheeks, burning a little when the wind picked up.

Last time, Mom had made me wait outside until Daddy was asleep on the couch with empty cans of beer around him. I knew what it was because he told me to get them for him out of the fridge lots of times. I'd had to stay out for so long that time.

Mom said the drinks either made him crazy or sleepy. I wanted sleepy, and I bet she did too. When they fought before, it hadn't been as cold. I hoped he went to sleep soon.

The freezing plastic seat of the swing bit into my legs as I sat there, twisting this way and that. Maybe if I went in and got him some more of the cans he liked, it might help. I half stood then froze, remembering that once when I'd done that, he'd pushed me. I didn't feel so good after that, and Mom had cried harder. I would stay outside.

I curled my hand around the chain, leaning against it, waiting. The wind was at my back, pushing my long hair over my shoulders. I wiped under my nose with my mitten and hoped my mom would come to the door and wave me in.

It was so cold. I shivered. The neighbors had a playhouse at the top of their swing set, and there wasn't a fence blocking me. I crossed to their yard and climbed inside.

I woke with a scream lodged in my throat and my skin slick with sweat. The dreams were back. *No, not dreams. Nightmares. Goddamn you, Charles!*

Several seconds passed while I regulated my breathing, grateful the flashback ended when and where it had. But I knew it would progressively get worse, and the rest would invade my mind with shocking clarity.

With shaky fingers, I untangled the sheet from my legs then swung them over the bed's side. I had to get up and watch TV or read for a while until the past receded.

Minutes or hours later—I couldn't be sure—I crawled back

in bed, exhausted. The memories had faded, and Charles occupied my thoughts.

———

FRIDAY MORNING, my mind still reeled from the nightmare, and I couldn't stop worrying that Charles would do something stupid —he'd looked so angry on Wednesday.

I was in dire need of meeting Ava for lunch and having some girl time.

I checked to be sure that my iPad was in my bag before swinging it over my shoulder. Locking the door to my apartment behind me, I shoved the anxiety away over how personal the two break-ins and that attack on the street felt. I needed to remember to call the police to see if there had been any progress with the investigation, but not yet. Jaxon had promised to get to the bottom of it, and I had to let it go and trust him. Otherwise, even more of the benefits from years of intense counseling would go down the drain.

The walk downtown did me some good, and my mood had lifted by the time I arrived at the café. As soon as Ava spotted me, she grinned and waved me over.

I sat across from her and leaned back against my chair, surveying her. She looked as she always did, perfectly put together. But then her bright-blue eyes flashed something that resembled concern as her smile fell away.

I wasn't ready to talk about everything yet and yanked my iPad from my bag, pasting a wide smile on my face. "I have your pictures."

"Oh! Let me see." Ava leaned forward, her hand extended.

I pulled the first one up and handed it over, glad she was effectively distracted, at least for a while. The waiter stopped by, and I ordered an iced tea—I'd decided to cut down on my coffee consumption, which was hard, given my job.

I nibbled on my lip for a second, hoping she would like them. I had my doubts, though. Something was off. They hadn't turned out how I'd hoped.

"I love them." Ava sighed, lifting her gaze to mine. "These are so much better than my current ones. Can you send them to me?"

"Absolutely." I had them ready on my phone just in case, and after a few taps, hers chimed. "They're in your inbox."

"I want to pay you for them."

"Sure. Buy me lunch." I thanked the waiter as he dropped my tea off, and we placed our orders while we had him there.

"That's not enough."

"You're my friend. I'm not charging you." I changed the subject because I wasn't up for arguing. "How was your trip?"

"So good. I received a lot of interest, and my agent is speaking to a few publishers already. Not only that, but I picked up another new client to get their employee manuals and technical procedures written. Going to lunch is keeping me from refreshing my email every second."

"Congratulations! I'm happy for you."

"Thanks." Ava leaned back, her gaze narrowing. "Now, tell me what happened while I was gone. How are you doing after finding out that Charles is married?"

A Koa butterfly fluttered by then landed on a nearby flower. The underside of its turquoise wings was visible until it fanned them out and took flight. The iridescent blue on the top of its wings sparkled in the sunlight. They were beautiful butterflies, and I had loads of pictures of them already.

"Better. It's still hard to believe."

"Are you going to find her, tell her about his affair?"

"No." I was horrified at even the thought of talking to his wife. "What if my telling her causes them to get a divorce?"

Ava grimaced. "I'll never leave my husband." She took a bite of her salad. "I won't let him leave me, either."

I spooned some soup into my mouth, contemplating her response. "I don't think I could trust my husband again if I found out he'd cheated. So no, I won't contact his wife. If she's aware of his infidelity, it would be like rubbing salt in the wound."

"I'm truly sorry."

With a shrug, I exchanged my spoon for the half sandwich. "It's over. I haven't made up my mind, but I may move after graduation."

Her brows furrowed. "To another apartment or out of Hawaii?"

"I'm for sure moving out of my apartment. As for staying in Hawaii, that's what I haven't decided yet."

"It'll work out." She reached across the table and squeezed my hand. "Why don't you stay at my place until you make that decision? At least there, you wouldn't have to worry about anyone breaking in."

"I appreciate it—you know I do—but I'm going to stay where I'm at." I didn't want to be a third wheel.

"On another note, I have to fly out again for about a week."

"What? You just got back." I scrunched my nose. "You were going to have me stay at your place, and you wouldn't even be there?"

Ava flashed a dazzling smile. "You can still do that, or you can fly out with me. I have a suite. There's plenty of room."

I shook my head. "I'll be fine. Promise. But thank you for the offer."

She squeezed my hand across the table. "You can change your mind about either offer any time, and we'll make it work."

The waiter appeared, and she took the bill from him, making him wait while she dug cash out to pay for it. "Back to why I'm leaving again so soon. My agent wants to take advantage of all the positive interest from the last conference. I was able to schedule a meeting with that new client I just told you about, but I'm hesitant to leave you alone after everything that's happened. I'll call and check on you to make sure everything is okay. And you do the same. Deal?"

I reluctantly agreed. Between her career, my graduate project, working at the Coffee Hut, and dating Xander, we hadn't had a lot of time to hang out. I missed her.

The walk home was uneventful and relaxing. I got my mail and discovered a package. Once inside, I opened it and found the book I'd ordered, *The Spider's Prey,* by Ava's favorite author.

I got settled on the lanai and traced my fingers over the raised silver spiderweb set against an orange background. The tagline was what had snagged my attention after the cover: *He's mine—until death.* With a few hours until I planned to work on editing photos, I started reading and was hooked from the very first line: "John held my hands in his as I repeated our wedding vows, a promise I would fulfill until the very end."

18

RILEY

Saturday afternoon, the click of the shutter vied for sonic dominance over the waves breaking against the sandy shoreline on Xander's family's private island. Xander walked out of the ocean like a mythological god with that mesmerizing, lethal sensuality that my camera and I loved. A lazy grin stretched across his face, beads of water clung to his tempting sun-kissed skin, and my stomach clenched with need.

Fighting the urge to throw myself at his sexy-as-hell body, I kept the lens trained on him for a few minutes longer even after he sat on the towel beside me, looped his arms over bent knees, then angled his head, his gaze meeting mine through the equipment's barrier. God, he was gorgeous, and the camera loved him. The scary thing was, I could see myself doing the same.

So many times, my mind drifted to all the times he'd kissed me. I hoped he would again. I blinked behind the lens and gave myself a mental shake back to the present.

"You don't mind, do you?" I lowered the camera. The urge to immortalize him through pictures had been too great when he emerged from the waves.

He shook his head. I snapped a few more then scrolled

through them, checking to see how they turned out. Zooming in on a few, even briefly, I could tell that the impression he'd given me from the start shone through in the frames. There was nothing sinister lurking in his emotions or body language.

It was silly that I relied on viewing the world through the camera lens to glean insight, but things were clearer to me that way. With my history, I didn't fully trust my instincts when it came to relationships.

"Tell me more about your brothers."

"Not much to tell. What exactly did you want to know?"

I wanted to learn more about him. "Are they like you?"

"Well, you met Jaxon. I would say he's a bit of a know-it-all." He grinned. "He would say that's because he's older and wiser."

I shaded my eyes, mirroring his pose with my other arm looped around my bent legs. "You don't get along, then?"

"We do. The police thing is weird, but Jaxon was master-at-arms early in his Navy career before joining the SEALs. Now, I think he's in limbo. He was injured and received an honorable discharge. And this police stuff is a test to see if it's the career he wants going forward. So far, he's not convinced. Part of the reason I'm fixing the cabins is that he's thinking of moving to our island and selling his condo."

"And you?" There were four cabins. I assumed one was for their parents. It made sense.

"I'm selling my condo, so yeah. Tyler will, too, or that's the plan, anyway."

I looked behind me at the houses, which were set back from the beach and surrounded by mature palm trees. They weren't precisely cabins. On the outside, they looked basic enough but with very cool upper and lower decks and lanais on the bottoms. They were large, and at least one of the houses looked like it had a hot tub on the lower deck. Inside, the spaces were much larger and more luxurious than they appeared.

"What will you do when you move here?" I could imagine

living on a private island. It was an introvert's fantasy. "Oh, wait. You're in the military."

"For now." His expression turned pensive, and he hesitated for a moment. "My contract is up for renewal soon, and I haven't decided what to do. Which is weird because I thought I would stay in until retirement, like our dad."

I dug my heels back and forth in the sand. "What will you do if you don't re-enlist? Or whatever it's called."

He smiled. "For now, Jaxon and I are toying with building a workshop here to make custom surfboards."

That was going to be a significant change from the excitement he probably experienced as a SEAL. "Won't you miss the action?" Given the great shape he was in, I had a hard time seeing him content with island life.

"I won't give it up completely. Jaxon has a buddy who works in private security contracting, mainly rescue and recovery. I've met the guys and like them. We'll take jobs here and there when Jack or anyone else from Gray Ghost Securities needs extra bodies."

"So it'll be similar to what you do now?"

"Pretty much. They're mostly former SEALs too. But I haven't made a decision one way or the other. It'll be there when I do." He leaned over and tucked a piece of long hair that'd come loose from my bun behind my ear.

At his touch, all thoughts scattered. Heat followed in the wake of his fingers as he trailed them along my cheek. My eyelids were heavy, and my breath hitched. As he shifted and cupped the back of my neck, applying gentle pressure, my gaze dropped to his lips. He met me halfway. I melted against his well-defined chest, my hand clinging to his shoulder as his mouth moved hungrily against mine.

A breathy moan escaped my lips when he shifted and hooked a hand under my thigh, lifting me to straddle him. My knees settled on either side of his hips, and my bikini-clad breasts brushed against his chest. His hand skimmed my thigh, moving higher, leaving goose bumps in its wake. I arched against him, and my hair tumbled down my back.

He gripped my waist, and a growl rumbled his throat, spurring my need to touch him, to explore the ridges and valleys of his muscles. He pulled me close, and I skimmed my fingertips over taut pecs and broad shoulders then threaded my fingers through his short hair. I altered the angle of the kiss and ground against the long, swollen length I felt at the apex of my thighs.

When his hand found my breast and rolled the peak, I hissed in pleasure, putty in his hands. He deepened the kiss, holding me tightly against him so I couldn't increase the heady friction by rocking my hips against him.

The tempo of the kiss changed, and the frantic, burning heat eased to smoldering until he broke the connection between our lips. We worked to catch our breath, and I mourned the loss of his mouth on mine. It took several minutes until we gained a semblance of control.

The shock of what could have happened and how far I would've let him go was what brought me back to reality. The rhythmic ebb and flow of the waves breaking against the shore and the intoxicating scent of hibiscus and coconut filtered back.

It wasn't like me to sleep with someone so soon or even to let passion take me away to the extent it had. But with him, I had very little restraint. All it took was a look or one touch of his hand, and I was lost. That thought should have terrified me, but oddly enough, it didn't.

———

THE SUN HAD DROPPED below the horizon an hour before, and I couldn't stop thinking about being with Xander earlier. I lay on my stomach on my bed, the cell phone pressed against my ear as

Ava worked to pry every detail from me about my day with Xander.

"That was it? You only kissed?" Ava harped. "You were on a private island, for Christ's sake."

I couldn't help but laugh. "He was the one to pull back. I'd lost all rational thought. Which was weird."

"What's weird about that? You have seen him, right? Or do you need glasses?" She snorted. "No woman would stand a chance against a drool-worthy hunk like him."

"You're married, right?"

"Married but not blind." Ava snickered. "I can fantasize virtually through you. Now, give me some better details."

She was more animated then normal, and I laughed as I asked her, "Are you drinking?"

"A little. I ordered a glass or three of wine with room service."

Room service sounded good—no cooking and delivery to the door. Even so, there was no way I was encouraging her with details about my date. "That's it. Just a kiss. The rest of the time, we surfed or walked along the shore. It was peaceful, relaxing." And intoxicatingly enjoyable whenever he touched any part of me. "We had sandwiches for lunch. Seriously, it was low-key."

"You're not telling me everything. Are you secretly in his bedroom and lying to me about it?"

"Oh my God, Ava! I'm in my apartment. Alone. We're taking things slow." *Or trying to.* At that point, I didn't trust myself. I wanted to throw caution to the wind. I guessed there was a first time for everything, as no other man had ever made me feel like Xander did. I needed a change of subject. "When are you coming home?"

A long, suffering sigh filtered through from her end. "Saturday. In time for your graduation."

"About that." I wasn't sure what her opinion would be, especially with her filters lowered by her wine consumption. "I'm not going."

I pulled my laptop over and logged in to my school account while we talked, and I waited for Ava to digest my last bit if news. A quick scan of my emails and I found one from the TA for Charles's class. I confirmed the time and date he'd set up for the test then logged back out.

There were several seconds of silence before she spoke, her voice lacking the teasing edge from earlier. "Don't let one asshole dictate your actions or take away from missing out on an experience you'll regret later."

My eyes blurred, and I rubbed at them with my free hand. "I'm not. I won't regret skipping it. I only would if I didn't receive my degree."

"You can't let any man mandate what you want out of life. They should fall in line with your goals." Ava's voice hardened. "It's your destiny, your ultimate choice for the future you want. *That* should be the lesson learned from dating the professor."

Something good had come out of dating Charles. I'd learned exactly what I wanted and found it with Xander. He was the future I wanted.

19

RILEY

I was tired as I trudged up the last few steps to the third floor after a short Sunday shift at the Coffee Hut. My legs ached from all the surfing and swimming Xander and I had done the day before. He wanted me to go today, too, but I couldn't because of work.

Footfalls sounded as someone ran up the stairs behind me. My legs shook, and I froze, unsure where to go or whether it would be best to dive inside my apartment or run. I waited like a deer in headlights, my breath caught in my throat as the noise came closer. Melanie exited the stairwell, and I sagged against my door, the thought of why she was there slow to come.

Cropped tawny hair swung around her pretty face, barely brushing her shoulders. A timid smile curved her lips, and she offered a small wave. "Hey, I hope you don't mind that I followed you, but I wanted to talk to you."

"I don't mind. Did you want to come in?" I waved at my door, hoping she would say yes.

"No. This will only take a second, and I have homework to finish."

I waited for her to continue, curious about what she was doing.

"I wanted to apologize to you about calling you a slut. I really liked Charles, and when I found out you were dating him, too, it was too much. I mean, I love him."

Oh crap. "I'm not dating him anymore, Melanie. But you know he's married, right?"

"I do. That doesn't mean that my feelings are gone, though." Her hazel eyes were rimmed with tears, and she sniffed. "Anyway, I've got to run, but it was bothering me that I let things get out of hand. Forgive me?"

"Sure. I'll see you at work."

She gave me another wave and brushed a rogue tear away as she hurtled back into the stairwell. I pushed out a breath and urged myself to face my apartment again. My hand shook as I reached for the doorknob, giving myself a stern lecture that everything would be all right. But the break-ins were always in the back of my mind. I wondered who it had been and if they were coming back or waiting for me inside.

Maybe I should have called off of work and stayed the weekend with Xander. Aside from the balcony, my place wasn't a sanctuary any longer. Anxiety spiked every time I came home. I took several deep breaths before I let myself enter.

Once inside, I shut and locked the door behind me then did a scan from corner to corner. It looked okay and like no one had been there. But the damage to my psyche had been done, and black spots danced in my peripheral vision. I dropped onto a chair and put my head between my legs until the feeling passed. The push and pull to go into my apartment but not wanting to had been too similar to what had happened to me before. The memories I most dreaded kept trying to resurface.

I shoved out of the chair and went in search of my book for a distraction. I couldn't deal with the memories of any part of that day from when I was young. I grabbed a glass of water and the book and headed to the lanai. It was the only place I liked to be, the most comfortable place in my violated apartment.

I sat, flipped the book open to where I last left off, and got to reading. I could see why Ava liked it so much. The tension was high, and the characters were likable so far—I had a feeling that would soon change. But it was nice to get lost in the fictional married couple and their quaint existence in a cookie-cutter neighborhood.

Even though the characters were happy, and things seemed innocent, I knew that everything would change, given the tagline and book description.

After several chapters, my eyelids drooped, and exhaustion settled in. In my sleep, it was harder to stave off the past. Images flooded my mind, taking me back to that cold day when my mom told me to stay outside until she called me back in.

I'd huddled in the corner of our neighbor's backyard playhouse and grew a tiny bit warmer without the wind pummeling me. It was quieter there, but I could still hear the shouting from my house. My stomach hurt, and I wanted my mom.

A loud boom echoed through the back of the house, spilling out from the weathered cracks in the siding and from the gap under the back door. Jerking to my feet, I took a step forward, unsure. The urge to run had me in a choke hold. Another ear-piercing crash split the silence. *Mom?* Her warning to stay outside evaporated, and I raced from the sheltered playhouse to the back door and yanked it open.

I skidded to a halt in the kitchen. Broken pieces of glass crunched under my boots. There was a red substance on the door that went into the TV room, like one of my finger paints but smeared. It smelled like the pennies Mom and I used to play with for a counting game, but that wasn't it. My teeth chattered as my body quaked violently. Something warm soaked down the inside of my jeans. Fear held me to the same spot. I wanted my mom.

There was no noise. I had to be quiet. She wouldn't be mad that I peed my pants. But he would. I tiptoed to the door, not wanting to touch it or to see what was on the other side.

I jerked in my chair, and the book in my lap fell with a thump. I sucked air into my lungs like a drowning victim. A warm breeze dried my wet cheeks. The distant roll of cresting waves further soothed my frantic mind, reminding me that my memory happened in the past. I was in Hawaii, safe from the memories. My gaze dropped to the book, and I retrieved it from the floor and set it on the table beside me.

It had taken so long to absolve myself of thinking that if I'd only gone inside when Dad told me to, Mom would still be alive.

My therapist had urged me to meditate in times of stress, if possible, to keep the flashbacks at bay. After years of counseling and practicing the poses, it had helped so much that I had been able to move forward and live my life free of guilt and pain. The experience was centering. I had time. The images were progressively getting worse, and I knew what I would see soon if I didn't calm down and strengthen my mental barriers.

After about a half hour of meditation on my screened-in balcony, I felt marginally better. I curled back up on my chair, letting the sound of the waves soothe me. Even with the balmy air and lush Hawaiian scenery, I felt empty, alone, and nostalgic —not a good combination. I shifted so that my knees were tucked beneath me and picked up my phone. It was a weak moment, and I knew it, but I did it anyway. I unblocked Charles.

The phone lit up as a slew of texts from that morning downloaded. I skimmed them. Some were apologetic. My stomach clenched at the futility of it all. I texted back *wife* then reblocked him.

Seconds passed. I thought responding would make me feel better. I didn't. Instead, the emptiness expanded, ushering in a sense of drowning. It wasn't that I wanted to get back together.

It was the loss of the friendship that we'd shared. I lurched from my chair and paced the length of the outdoor space.

I needed to get a grip on my erratic thoughts. Worrying my lower lip, I picked up my cell again, wondering whether I would seem desperate if I called Xander. *Screw it.* I pressed his contact and put the phone to my ear. I was balancing on the edge, and hearing his voice would chase away all of the day's unpleasantness.

He answered on the third ring. "Hey, Riley. I'm glad you called."

I grinned at the genuine happiness I heard in his voice. "What are you up to?" I wanted him to tell me he was in the neighborhood, and that he would stop by, but I didn't think that was likely.

"Inspecting a roof and making plans for the repair."

"Ah, on your family's island. I bet it's gorgeous there today."

"It is. The waves are begging for us to ride them. You should come by. Say the word, and I'll pick you up."

"I want to, but..." I sighed but gave in to the fantasy. "Sweeten the deal with a piña colada after we've spent a couple hours in the water, and I'm there."

He laughed, and I shivered at how his voice worked over every inch of me.

"That could be arranged."

I wish. But we both had stuff to get done. We talked for an hour. He invited me to the island on Friday with the option to stay the weekend. He was persuasive and charming as usual, and I agreed. If I wanted to come back in time for graduation, then I would. I wasn't sure I wanted to, though, as Charles would be there too.

With that heavy thought, I packed up my stuff from the veranda and went inside for the night. I had just enough energy to make a sandwich then climb into bed.

2 0

RILEY

Monday afternoon, I met with Charles's TA and took the last exam. The TA promised to let me know the score I got on the test. Then all I had to do was pay close attention to my grades to make sure Charles didn't pull anything. Graduation was the following Sunday.

Most grad students were in a frenzy, turning in their assignments and studying for whatever tests or quizzes remained. I was thankful for the photography experience I had already. It gave me a leg up and took most of the stress away. I was used to working hard to make ends meet when I was in college, hustling for representation, and editing late into the night. Grad school was still difficult, but it was manageable for me.

There were only a few more touch-ups to do on my grad project, then the portfolio would be complete. I would turn it in early the next morning, and then I was officially done. I'd decided not to attend the graduation ceremony and thought about celebrating with shopping on Sunday instead.

The timer beeped on the oven, and I took out a single-serving lasagna. I'd skipped breakfast, running late to cover my last shift at the Coffee Hut. Jeffery had found someone with

140

barista experience who could start right away and gave me the option to fulfill my two weeks or not. I went with not.

I was lucky that he, Chloe, and I were friends, and that he was cool about my leaving. College students were always looking for work, and he had applications piling up on his desk, anyway. It all worked out.

The only thing that hadn't sat right with me was when they'd both asked if I'd heard from Mel. Apparently, she hadn't shown for her shift, and they hadn't been able to reach her. It was odd but no longer my problem, and I put it from my thoughts.

The smell of Italian food filled my small kitchen, and my mouth watered. With my food on a plate and the oven off, I settled at the peninsula and dug in. A light mist and thick gray clouds darkened the sky, and my mind strayed to my phone call with Xander from the night before.

I wouldn't have minded watching him while he worked on the house. I'd already had the pleasure of witnessing him on a surfboard. The image was permanently seared into my brain.

Spending the weekend with him was a big step. My body temperature shot up with the thought, and I could barely make myself wait until Friday. But if I wanted to go—and I did—I would have to finish everything on my end first.

After cleaning up the dishes, I got to work on editing the last few pictures of the flowers I'd taken the day Charles accosted me on campus. My stomach clenched at the thought of that last confrontation and the texts, and I took a few deep breaths. His desperation to keep things going didn't make sense. Even though I hadn't known about his wife, the guilt over dating a married man was enough to keep me far away. Unblocking him the day before, even for that short amount of time, had been a mistake I wouldn't repeat.

An hour passed, and I finished with my grad project. With everything in order and ready to deliver the next morning, I had free time to read. I picked up the hardcover book and immediately got lost in the pages. Chills raised the tiny hairs on the back of my neck.

Damn him. I swiped at the tear that escaped. Did I mean so little to him? The blinds slipped from my fingers from the empty office building across from his. I crossed my arms tight over my waist. Married for two years, and this was the thanks I got? I peeked through the metal slats. The young blond intern had her hand on his bicep as she leaned into him, her head tilted invitingly. He dipped his head down, and I staggered back a step. He kissed her!

Fury boiled in my gut, and my nails cut crescent moons into my arms. We'd taken vows. He was mine.

I stood frozen at the window, watching them.

I would make her pay. She would come to realize that she'd tres-passed. My lips twitched. Not yet. I wanted to play with her a little.

A plan took shape, and I giggled. I didn't mind the game I would take part in. Someone had to teach them both a lesson and remind Brad of his promise.

One week had passed since I'd first spotted the little home-wrecker. Men were weak. I partially expected something like this. The problem was that I hadn't thought it would happen so soon. No matter. In her apartment building, I shifted to the balls of my feet, ready for the perfect moment.

I'd learned her routine while Brad was busy at his dental practice. I worked part-time in billing, making sure the hygienists knew who I was. They thought I was kind, caring. It was the image I wanted them to have. The interns weren't there on the days I was, which was prob-ably by Brad's design.

After I found out about their affair, I hacked his phone and installed an app that would let me see any messages he sent. They communicated often. Today, they planned to spend a few hours together because I would be at book group. She'd told him to bring wine, and that she would be the dessert. Stupid and cliché. Did she have no imagination?

It wasn't hard to find out where she lived. When she was expected home, early evening, I hid in the apartment complex close to where she would round one floor then climb the next.

Her perky voice carried up the stairs while she chatted on the phone. My fingers tightened around the bat. I was ready. Blond ponytail swinging, she came closer. I dropped a penny. It bounced down the steps, distracting her. She pivoted with her gaze on the penny, not me.

I swung. The bat connected with her shoulder then clipped part of her head. She flew back, and her feet left the ground. Her cell phone flipped through the air. An ear-piercing scream echoed off the walls as she tumbled down the stairs to land, unmoving in a heap at the bottom.

People would've heard. I slipped the bat under my long trench coat, grateful for the misting rain, so it didn't look out of place. My feet were soundless as I sped down the steps. I stepped over her unconscious form, pausing long enough to feel for a pulse at her neck.

She was alive.

No one would know who had pushed her down the stairs.

Doors opened in the building as I slipped out the front door. On the sidewalk, I blended in with a couple of people hurrying to their destinations with their heads bent against the weather. Phone in hand, I pressed Brad's number and waited for him to pick up.

He didn't. But his voicemail did, and I added extra sugar to my voice, so he didn't hear the satisfaction I masked as I left a message. "Hi, honey. Book group was canceled tonight because Betty isn't feeling well. I thought we could go to dinner and a movie. I made reservations at your favorite place. I'll meet you there at six." After disconnecting, I dialed his practice then left a similar message with his receptionist and a reminder for him to check his messages.

I had enough time to stop at home, freshen up, wash off, and hide the bat.

I slipped my phone back into my purse and grinned. This wasn't the end of things with Blondie. I had more lessons to teach them.

It wouldn't be long before Brad remembered the ironclad vow he'd made to me.

Unsettled, I closed the book and set it aside. It was hard to stop. The tension and uncertainty of what would happen next made me want to keep going, but being alone fed into my jitteriness from the post-traumatic memories I fought and the drama with Charles. No, I would wait to read more when I was somewhere I felt safe, which was with Xander.

I tugged at the hem of my T-shirt, toying with an idea. It was bold, but I was going for it. I sent him a text saying I would be free earlier this week and could come to the island as soon as Wednesday, if that worked.

A few minutes later, he responded. I grinned from ear to ear because he'd said yes. He would be back in Honolulu tonight and would meet me tomorrow at the harbor. With school, work, and meeting Xander, my life was finally looking up.

XANDER

I had been lounging on one of Jaxon's balcony chairs when my phone rang. I pressed the cell against my ear, pinpricks of warning stilling all further movement. Mark's voice jolted me into an upright position. Jaxon's hand, which held his beer, paused halfway to his mouth. It was clear that he, too, sensed from the tension in the air that it wouldn't be good news.

"I tried to get ahold of Tyler earlier today but couldn't," Mark whispered. "Daryl pulled the reports from the last mission. I don't know what's up, but he's going over them with a few guys on your team. I overheard that he might send Tyler on another mission."

"Why haven't I been called in?" It wasn't normal. Even if I wasn't needed for the mission, I should have been included in the meeting. After years of working together, our team was tight.

"I don't know. The thing that caused a red flag is that no new messages have come in. We don't have another informant, but he's acting like he has new intel."

"Fuck. I'll find a reason to come in. Is Tyler there?"

"Yes." Commotion sounded on his end. "I've gotta go. Maybe check with Tyler before doing anything."

"Yeah, will do. Thanks for the heads-up."

Mark disconnected, and my gaze locked with Jaxon's. He didn't pretend he hadn't heard every word, which saved me from explaining the conversation with Mark. "I've got a bad feeling about this."

"It doesn't make sense why you aren't there. We'll have to wait to hear from Tyler." Jaxon rocked back in his chair like our brother Ty did, balancing precariously. "You're right."

I summed up the call and a meeting that hadn't included me. "There isn't any news about a new mission." That was all I could really say, even though he was my brother and a former SEAL. If they'd gotten new intel on where the weapons were, I hadn't heard anything about it.

"If what you're going for there is even there."

I side-eyed Jax. "Come on."

"Yeah." He grunted. "Whatever it is, it's there. I was just hoping that for once, things were good."

"I can't sit around anymore. I need to go back on base."

"Normally, I would agree." Jaxon dropped the front legs of his chair back down and set his beer beside the empty burger wrappers from lunch. "But Ty's there. Let him ferret out information. He's good at that. Then you can reconvene with him and figure out what the hell is going on."

I didn't like it, but he had a point. Ty was damn good at putting together missing puzzle pieces.

"How much personal time do you have left?"

I rolled my eyes. "The enforced leave? I've got another week." I was pissed about it, but on the flip side, I'd met Riley, and she was worth any aggravation from Daryl. "It's bullshit, though. Daryl put in for it. I can't help but wonder if he did it to get me out of the way."

Riley

I COULDN'T WIPE the grin off my face as I rounded the corner and hurried to my apartment. All the work was done, and my grad project was in my professor's hands. I'd checked my grade for my theory test—I got an A. After taking a screenshot of it, just in case, I was good. Not only that, but my diploma would be in the mail after the weekend. I wouldn't have to go to campus again. The relief was tangible and nailed home how much the conflict with Charles had affected me.

The best part was that I was going to spend more time with Xander soon.

I shoved the heavy stairwell door open then turned the corner of the hallway to where my third-story apartment was. The smell of copper, like old pennies but not, hit me, and my reaction was instantaneous. Bile climbed my throat in a bitter, acidic burn.

It was familiar. Jarring. Horrifying. My heart rate accelerated as if I was sprinting, and I wanted to—I felt an impulse to get away from there and from what I feared I would see. *Again.* My lungs strained to pull in a full breath, but I crept closer.

There was no telltale sound of anyone home on my floor as I inched past a few closed doors in the dim hallway. I wished my neighbors weren't at work or out. If they had been there, movement or muffled voices would have indicated their presence. Panic surged, and I broke into a cold sweat. No one could save me if the attacker was still there. I crept closer, helpless against the pull of what waited for me. Dread sat heavily in my gut.

Something coated the doorknob. An ominous drip landed on the floor, runoff from the liquid that had been thrown against the worn but solid wood. I took a half step back as I gagged. A wretched, acidic taste coated my tongue, and tears streamed from my eyes. My hands trembled as I pulled my phone from my pocket, refusing to look at the knife that jutted from the door, anchoring the paper below it.

Is someone inside? My heart leapt to my throat, and the shaking in my limbs intensified. I couldn't make out the words on the paper beyond the tears swimming in my eyes. I blinked furiously, letting them fall over my lashes in an attempt to clear my vision. I took one step back then another. I could make it to the stairwell—to safety.

I knew who I wanted to call, who made me feel safe. But it would take too long for him to rescue me. I called Xander anyway. My fingers found my cell phone in my pocket, and I pulled it out. I instantly pressed Xander's number as I inched farther along the hall, stopping three feet away from my door.

Bile climbed my throat as Xander answered. I choked out that I needed him.

"What's wrong?" he asked.

"There's blood. And a-a—" I couldn't get it out. The knife wasn't something I had personal experience with. The blood— God, yes. And I was terrified about what it meant.

"Where are you?"

His strong, take-charge voice pierced my consciousness and spurred my legs into motion. I backed away, pivoted, then fled down the stairs. "Home. On the stairs now."

"I'm half an hour away. I'll call Jaxon. He can get there sooner. Go outside, Riley, or into someone's apartment that you know."

"Going." As if my feet had wings, I was out the door and on the sidewalk in a matter of seconds. The phone went back into my pocket, and I bent at the waist, gasping for breath.

Sweat coated my hands and beaded along my hairline and upper lip. The memories were close. I was both hot and cold, unable to control my body temperature or the shaking. It would get worse. I had to get help before the past caught up to me in more ways than one.

My stomach cramped, and I wanted to curl into a ball on the cement. Instead, I leaned against the building, hands on my knees. The damage was done. I couldn't stop the childhood memories from crowding back, and they exploded into my mind with the viciousness of a sledgehammer.

The scent of old pennies saturated the air, and I gagged. It was familiar, evoking horror and nausea. Loneliness. Abandonment.

What else will be taken from me?

At seven years old, I'd grasped a doorknob, and the sticky stuff had gotten on my skin. I yanked my hand back, not wanting to see what was on the other side of the door. There was no one else there. I had to.

My fingers gripped the knob to our back door, and I pushed.

As the sight I'd seen in my youth invaded my mind, I jolted violently from the memory. Gasping, my heart thudded painfully, and I found myself on the ground. I wildly glanced around, cataloging my surroundings. Palm fronds rustled overhead, and cars zoomed by on the street. The cloudless sky and warm breeze were so very different from that day. It wasn't my childhood home. I was in Hawaii—*safe.*

The high-pitched whine of a siren preceded flashing red and blue lights. Jaxon slammed the police cruiser to a halt at the curb. He unfurled himself from the car and rose to his impressive six-foot-plus height, carrying himself so similarly to Xander.

"Riley?" He approached cautiously. "Are you okay? Can you tell me what happened?"

Warm brown eyes met mine as I relayed the details of coming home and finding the blood and the knife.

"Was anyone there?"

I shook my head. "I don't think so. I didn't wait to find out."

"Good." Xander's pickup truck screeched to a stop behind Jaxon's squad car. "Hang tight while I go have a look."

Jaxon disappeared inside the building as Xander hopped out and was by my side in a heartbeat. When he opened his arms, I fell into his embrace, soaking up the strength and security, the warmth. There were things I would have to face, like who was behind the incident upstairs and why. It was too similar with what I'd already experienced. For the time being, though, I preferred to let Xander keep the world at bay.

More police cars came to a halt, lining up behind the two vehicles parked at the curb. Xander exchanged a word with some of them while my eyes stayed shut, blocking out the team that would comb through my apartment.

"I can't do this."

"Darlin', you don't have to be afraid. I'm right here by your side."

I leaned into him until Jaxon came down, maybe an hour later. My fingers tightened on Xander's black T-shirt. I held very still, unwilling to leave the protection of his arms. The concern in Jaxon's eyes warned me that I wouldn't like what he had to say.

"We aren't finding evidence of any other prints than what was here last time. The detective on duty would like you to come to the station for questioning."

"Not today. She's been through enough. Not only that, but there are no grounds to have her go to the station." Xander stiffened against me as he leveled his brother with a penetrating gaze. "She stays with me."

XANDER

Flames danced in the makeshift bonfire pit, casting a golden glow on Riley's taut face. It'd taken some time to pack what she needed most from her apartment and move them to my island until things were sorted. There weren't any new prints inside. The handwriting on the note was similar to hers. Jaxon didn't think it looked good but hadn't said so—as my brother, I knew his tells, what he was thinking. While he was worried about her innocence, I was not.

Tremors wracked her slender frame, and I held her and encouraged her to take sips of ginger ale. Exhausted, she'd quieted and even dozed for a few minutes. I brushed a kiss across her forehead and carefully shifted her from my arms. Then I stood and stepped a couple feet away. I hadn't wanted to release her. But what I also wanted to do was hunt down whoever had done it. The protective instincts inside me had flared to a blazing inferno.

Without knowing it, she'd changed everything for me.

The fire flickered from a small gust of wind that swept along the beach. Palms rustled overhead, and night ushered in with a dramatic whoosh. I couldn't put it off any longer and called

Jaxon while Riley waited for me to return. I remained nearby, close enough so she could see me, so she would know she was safe.

"You'd better know what you're doing," Jaxon snapped as soon as he answered.

"I told you at her place. She stays with me." I hadn't liked the insinuation behind the questions the police had asked, and I'd acted on instinct. "She wasn't under arrest. Besides, you know it's safer for her if she's with me."

"I get it." Weariness clung to his words. "The detective is trying to use the angle that she's a suspect. We don't know whose blood—"

"It could have been from an animal."

"And the note, 'this isn't finished'? It's ambiguous. Not to mention the handwriting. Between this and the last call, the incidents appear staged."

"The key word there is 'similar,' and you know that's bullshit."

"Yeah, I do. And trust me, I'm on your side here. But I still shouldn't have let you two leave when you did. You knew things were going to go to hell and slipped away on purpose. Sending me a text and taking off with Riley was bullshit."

After Jaxon had given us a preliminary rundown of what the team had found, the cops had allowed us back into her apartment to recover any items she would need. The questioning began with the detective onsite, and my instincts screamed to get her out of there. Then we were told to wait outside while they locked up and went over a few theories—the detective issued a warning not to go anywhere. I ushered Riley into my truck and took off, texting Jaxon at a stoplight to tell him where we were headed.

"She hasn't done anything wrong, and there's no reason to lock her up while the investigation is going on."

"I agree. There were just a few questions the detective

wanted her to answer, which started when her prints were the only ones on the knife that was stuck in the door."

"Yeah, because it was hers, taken from her apartment."

"Even so, you're putting me in a bad position," Jaxon said. "I don't think she should be charged, either, but fleeing the scene didn't win any points with the detective assigned to the case. He's going to be a real pain in the ass. He doesn't always follow the best leads. If he catches wind of an easy thread, he'll pull, regardless of whether there's better, more accurate ones. It's always the path of least resistance with him."

I shook my head. "It's temporary. Isn't Chief Kane due to come back soon?"

"That's not the point." Silence stretched between us. "Remember that I'm pulling for you both, but we need to cover all angles. You don't know her that well. The pain-in-the-ass detective brought up a point about her recent breakup and the possibility that she's trying to draw attention to herself. It's something to consider. What if this is like all those cases where the husband killed his mistress? I can think of twelve off the top of my head. The soccer player murdering his girlfriend and feeding her to his dogs, the marine killing his girlfriend, the cop, or the principal—all to avoid getting caught by their wives. All these cases were about not getting caught. From what you told me, she and Charles broke up when she learned about his wife —could it be they were playing a deadly game with each other?"

"It's not her. Question the professor." I couldn't help the growl that came with the thought of her ex-boyfriend.

"We're looking into him as a potential suspect but haven't been able to reach him. Nor has the university or his wife. Charles Wright missing isn't the detective's only concern or angle. What if she killed Charles because he wouldn't leave his wife?"

"I'm not entertaining this stupidity. I called you to make sure we're good. I'm keeping her here with me."

"I'm not arguing she isn't safest with you. But know that you're damn lucky I'm involved with this case, or she'd be behind bars. Nolan, the head detective, is worried I'm gunning for his position. He's looking for an easy win here to shut me down. So far, he hasn't had good enough reason to come after her."

"So Riley is a scapegoat because of your involvement?" It sounded like this Nolan guy had a chip on his shoulder and a know-it-all attitude.

"Yeah, in a way."

Dammit, that meant he was targeting her despite any evidence that pointed elsewhere. "Keep Nolan away."

"I'm working on that. Keep Riley in your sight." Jaxon sighed when I didn't respond. "I'm not happy about this, either, but there are things that aren't adding up—like how we can't get ahold of the ex-boyfriend."

No matter what secrets Riley had, I knew she was innocent.

***

Riley

Delicious heat blanketed my back, and a heavy weight anchored me where I lay. The ebb and flow of the cresting waves eased me into the next day, and I cracked my eyes open. We were on the couch in Xander's oceanside lanai, and it was his arm thrown over my waist that kept me in place.

We'd stayed up late into the night, watching a storm roll in. Lightning had split the sky, and flashing sheets of rain fell while booming thunder vied for supremacy with the roar of the waves hurtling against the shore. The palm trees bent and shook their fronds in response to the gusting wind. Electricity charged the air. It was dark, but when lightning lit the sky, we glimpsed a water funnel dancing on the horizon.

It was a fitting end to a traumatic day.

Xander had relayed what Jaxon had told him about the prints on the knife being mine alone. They were waiting for forensics to tell them whether the blood was animal or human. But I suspected it would be human. Thinking about it made a panic attack threaten to come on. I took a few deep breaths and thought about Xander, which helped me take my mind off my problems.

Wrapped in his protective arms, the horror of the day before lost some of its tenacious grip on my psyche. He'd helped keep the monsters at bay, and I was able to stave off the fear for a little while. But there were things I had to tell him. As we'd hunkered down before the bonfire, he'd given me a reprieve. I couldn't wait any longer. He needed to know everything.

"Morning," Xander greeted.

I repressed a shiver from his sexy-as-sin morning voice. "Morning."

He moved his arm as I went to sit up. I stood and stretched. When I turned, he got to his feet, running his fingers through his hair. I located my bag on the chair near the screen door, unzipped it, then grabbed a few things to take to the bathroom, leaving the rest where it was because I wouldn't be staying in his house. He'd promised I could use the one closest unless I wanted to stay with him. I wasn't ready to, so next door was perfect. But I couldn't go anywhere until we talked. And for that, I needed a clear head. "Do you have any coffee?"

"I'll make us some." He waved to the inside portion of the house. "Make yourself at home. You remember where the bathroom is?"

"Yes. I'm good." I grinned because he was a whole other level of drool-worthy first thing in the morning, with those bedroom eyes and the hint of softness to such a powerful man. I scurried into the house and got to brushing my teeth and splashing water on my face. Five minutes later, I was back on the lanai, sitting in a single chair with my feet up on the ottoman when Xander came in with two large cups of coffee.

I thanked him and wrapped my hands around the hot mug, breathing in the rich scent of coffee beans and cream. We sat in silence for a few minutes, waiting for the caffeine to infuse our blood and for our synapses to start firing.

There was no hurry to talk. Xander didn't pressure me. But I couldn't put it off any longer. I couldn't see why my past and present were connected, but even so, he deserved an explanation for my post-traumatic responses after the nightmare. I was sure there would be more, as the night terrors were back in full force.

I gripped the warm mug, staring into its dark contents as I began. "I was seven years old when I went to live with my aunt. That day haunts my mind as the worst one in my life." I shivered despite the heat all around me. "It was cold. Late October in the Midwest. We'd gotten some snow earlier in the week, and the ground was frozen."

Xander sat motionless opposite me, his coffee probably growing cold. I was glad for the silence and for him letting me tell the story at my own pace.

"My parents were fighting again. They did that a lot, but it wasn't always bad. This was one of the times it was. I remember sitting at our white round table with its chips and scuff marks, eating a peanut-butter-and-jelly sandwich. The kitchen was at the back of the house, with a door that led to the backyard, and opposite it was another that went into the family room. That's where they were. There were a few minutes where there wasn't any screaming, and my mom came into the kitchen. I'll never forget the look in her eyes. She was frantic but trying to hide it while she bundled me up in my winter coat and boots and told me to go outside. I wasn't supposed to come back in unless she called me."

I lifted the coffee to my lips and took a few gulps, needing the strength to tell him the rest.

Xander waited for me to continue.

"I went to the swings, but it was windy and cold. They were shouting at each other again, and I almost went back inside, but there was the promise I'd made to my mom. So I didn't. My neighbors had a playhouse with their swing set, and since there wasn't a fence between our yards, I went there and huddled against the wall to try to stay warm until Mom called me inside.

"Dad yelled for me, but"—I shrugged—"I'd made a promise. I didn't go in. Not long after that, there was this deafening boom. I stood up then because I was worried and didn't know what I should do. There was another noise like the one before it. I ran inside, even though I wasn't supposed to. Blood has that weird smell." I met Xander's solemn gaze. He knew.

"There was red on the door between the kitchen and the family room, and I remember thinking that it looked a little like when I finger painted but messier. The handprints were smeared and long. When I got up the nerve to open the door, the blood got on my hands." I shuddered.

Xander's hand found my knee. "You don't have to keep going if you don't want to."

I gave him a weak smile. "It's okay, but maybe not all the details. They were dead in the other room, but I didn't accept it until much later. My aunt told me that my no-good, worthless dad killed my mom before turning the gun on himself. She also said that if my mom had left him and stayed away, as she had when I was a baby, she wouldn't have had to take me in."

He plucked the mug from my hands and set it on a table. Then his arms slid under my thighs and around my back. He lifted me onto his lap and cradled me against him. "It's a damn good thing you didn't go in when he called you."

Neither of us said anything after that statement. If I had listened to my dad, I would have died too.

We spent the rest of the day together, walking the shore and picking up shells. He told me stories of him and his brothers growing up, the trouble they got into, and how their strict but loving parents dealt with disciplining them. He said it rarely worked, but the physical labor made them stronger and more appreciative of one another—and oddly, of family. They were taxed with things like building a pier into the water on the island or digging trenches, but they always did so as a unit, working together to solve problems and execute solutions.

I appreciated the life he'd had while growing up and marveled at the differences between us. My past squatted in my mind, heavy and dark, draining me of energy.

But Xander offered the promise of a better tomorrow, a joyful future.

23

RILEY

The small duffel landed on the mattress next to the backpack with my camera equipment. I rubbed a weary hand over the back of my neck, emotionally drained from the conversation with Xander yesterday morning. It was hard to believe it was only Wednesday and that graduation was Sunday. There wasn't a shred of doubt about my decision not to go.

Xander had invited me to join him for a jog on the beach, but I'd declined. I needed some alone time to process everything. I pursed my lips. Along with my camera, I'd brought my laptop. I could work on putting together the cover letter and a sample of the pictures I wanted to send to the New York gallery. Or I could escape reality and get lost in *The Spider's Prey*. That was preferable. The heavy book in my bag beckoned, and I pulled it out then settled on the comfortable chair on the lanai in the cabin next door to Xander's. Kicking my feet up on the ottoman, I opened the book to where I'd left off.

The mix of greens hid the crushed pill added into the salad dressing. Brad wouldn't detect anything. We sat across from one another, and he asked me about my day with that irritating distracted smile. He wasn't thinking about me or focusing on what I was saying. I slipped in a few outlandish events, like how my friend Sylvia had shoplifted a lipstick then tripped over the store's metal threshold. She fell on the cement and sprained her wrist when she tried to break her fall. The nod and absent comment he gave was typical when his mind was elsewhere. He wasn't listening. He was thinking of her.

When his cell phone chimed and he excused himself to answer, I was able to hear every word—on his end. The call was planned.

He returned to the table, a predictable apology at the ready. "I'm sorry, sweetheart. I have to go in for a dental emergency."

"Do you have time to finish dinner? I made a pot roast."

"No. He's already on his way, and so is Ruth." He shoveled the last bite of salad in.

"Ruth does a wonderful job." I did like her, and the fact that she was much older was a bonus. "I'm glad she'll be there to assist you."

I stood and followed Brad to the door, admiring his broad shoulders. He paused before leaving and brushed my hair back, dropping a soft kiss on my lips.

I sighed. "I wish you didn't have to go."

"I'll only be a couple of hours."

Rather than answer, I drew him in for a hug. "Be careful."

The door clicked shut behind his retreating form, and seconds later, he pulled out of our garage. I watched the headlights of his silver BMW disappear, and my feeling of satisfaction brewed.

His stupid intern had a penchant for wine. The crushed medicine he'd consumed would react unfavorably with the tannins and alcohol in the red she preferred. I laughed as I pivoted on a heel then went to the kitchen to clean up.

While Brad would rather have a pilsner, I knew he indulged her in the wine by his blue-stained teeth after he was with her. A few sips tonight, and they would be on their way to the ER. I knew the nurse at the registration desk, the one Blondie would encounter when she tried to see him.

They were in for a nasty surprise.

I chuckled as I rinsed the dishes then started the dishwasher. What would she think after finding out he wasn't divorced? What would he do? I couldn't wait to find out.

Chills raced up my arms. I dropped the book and jumped from my seat, glaring at it for several minutes. *Holy hell!* Dark spots swam in my peripheral vision, and I blinked furiously to chase them away while sucking in deep, calming breaths.

The parallel with what had happened the night Charles had come to my apartment, trying to work things out, was too similar to discount. He'd had some wine, then heart-attack symptoms caused us to get him to the hospital quickly, where I learned he wasn't divorced, that he was married and had lied to me.

Melanie's unhealthy obsession with Charles and that she was a published author invaded my thoughts. *Could it be her?* I flipped the book so that the author's cover picture was visible. The image was blurry through cigarette smoke that dangled from crimson-painted lips—that lipstick was the only color in the grayscale portrait. Dark hair hung in straight lines on either side of an oval face, obscured by large black sunglasses. It was mysterious and alluring.

The professional in me admired the picture, but the part of me who related to a portion of the writer's plot was terrified. I told myself it was probably just my overactive imagination causing problems again—that had to be it. I closed the book and set it aside. Rather than stay in the house, I changed into a black bikini and went outside for some sun.

I spread a towel on the white sand, put my sunglasses on, and scanned the shore, trying to spot Xander jogging back. I could see him in the distance and braced myself on my elbows to wait, taking in the horizon. *Maybe surfing would be a good way to get my mind off things.* The waves were bigger on the northern end of the beach, but reefs were sticking out in one area, and I preferred to steer clear of that.

Something bobbed in the water, moving in conjunction with

the swells as they flowed around the jagged black rock. *What is that?* I stood, shaded my eyes, and squinted for a better view.

My mind pieced together the tattered fabric and lifeless appendages. As soon as it all merged into one cohesive image, I fell to my hands and knees. *No!* I dry heaved over and over, my limbs shaking uncontrollably. Warmth enveloped me, keeping me from falling. I recognized the deep voice in my ear. Xander was back, and he held me. I couldn't speak. Instead, I shuddered in his arms, and with a shaky finger, I pointed to the body that bobbed not too far from where we were sitting.

Something about the clothes registered. Navy tie—I knew who that was. What I didn't understand was why Charles's body had washed up on the island.

———

Xander

MY SHOES DUG into the sand as I jogged my way back to Riley, who paced franticly. The body caught in the reef wasn't bloated yet but looked to have been there for at least twelve hours. It was mostly intact, minus a foot that had marks on the ankle from shark teeth.

I grabbed Riley's hand then wrapped my arm around her as I went to retrieve my cell from inside to call Jaxon. After I got my phone, I guided her back outside to wait.

Toeing off the gym shoes that I'd worn while running, I grabbed a towel and sat in the sand with Riley, who hadn't spoken since I'd gone to get a better look at the body. *Christ.* These past two days had been hell for her.

I tugged her against my side. The phone rang twice before Jaxon's curt hello. I didn't waste words but got right down to the heart of the problem. "Think we found Charles. There's a body caught in the reef."

"Riley was with you since the incident yesterday?"

"Yes." The move into the house hadn't happened until after breakfast that morning.

"I'll call the Coast Guard. Nolan's working another case, but I've got to let him know about this."

"Do what you can, okay?" I had to ask even though I knew he would. It would be better if Jaxon questioned Riley, rather than someone else.

"I'll run interference with Nolan, but you know how he is."

I did, as Jaxon had gone into detail about what working with him was like.

"See if Tyler can stay on the island too."

"I can do that, but we tasked him with something else to look into."

Something crashed on the other end, and I could relate. We were in a bind. I'd put Jaxon in one by protecting Riley despite his need to have her close and interrogate her, and by asking him to keep Nolan on a leash as much as he could.

Our younger brother, Tyler, would have helped, but we had other issues—in particular, his pending deployment. In the back of my mind, I worried about him going and what could happen. We had to find that mole. And we would, but my immediate focus had to be on Riley and the trouble that kept finding her.

It didn't take long for the Coast Guard to arrive. Riley remained tucked into my side. Tremors wracked her frame, and even though I tried to keep her from seeing it, she cried out when the body was pulled from the water. Dead and missing a foot, it wasn't a pretty sight.

The Coast Guard loaded Charles onto the boat, and once he was able, Jaxon made his way to us. He had questions, but I would make sure it was a short visit. Riley had been through enough.

The wind pushed against us, blowing her dark hair away from her face. Thankfully, we were far enough away that the stench of the body wouldn't reach us. She gagged, no doubt from the visual of someone she knew being dragged from the ocean.

I kept my arm firmly around her as Jaxon approached, his hardened cop face intact. My gaze narrowed, and I promised retribution if he upset her further.

Jaxon stood before us, bracing his legs in the sand with his arms loose at his sides. "Hey, Riley, wish we were meeting again under better circumstances."

She cleared her throat. "I do too."

"Right now, we're operating under the assumption that your ex was attempting to reach you, as you said he hadn't taken your breakup well. Since it was storming the night before and there is no visible foul play, the theory is that his boat capsized before he made it here, and he drowned. It's the most likely scenario as of now."

"That makes sense, but it doesn't take away from how awful this is."

Jaxon grimaced. "There's more. The tox report came back, confirming that the blood on your door was human and not animal."

Her face leeched of more color, if that was possible, and a tremor went through her.

I rubbed her arm, securing her tighter to my side. "Do you know whose it was yet?"

Jaxson's attention swung to me. "No."

He wasn't saying more, but I knew they would test the blood against the body they had in their possession.

A muscle leapt in Jaxon's jaw as he met Riley's gaze. "I'm sorry to do this, but I need to ask you a few questions."

She scrubbed at tearstained cheeks as she lifted her chin higher and braced herself for what Jaxon would ask. "I understand. Go ahead."

I was furious at the situation. Riley remained glued to my side, leaning into me, taking the support I offered.

"I need to know your whereabouts since Monday." With his mouth pressed into a straight line, Jax's features were grim.

I took reassurance in that, as it was clear he didn't like this any more than I did.

"I spent Monday night in my apartment, alone. On Tuesday, I called for help when the blood and knife were found on my door. I've been with Xander ever since."

Jaxon held his cell phone in front of us of, a driver's license picture on the screen that showed a pretty woman with wild, shoulder-length curly hair, dark-brown eyes, a narrow nose, and high cheekbones. "This is Mrs. Wright. Do you recognize her?"

"No."

He squeezed her arm and offered a weak smile. "Thanks, Riley. Try not to worry. We're working round the clock to find out what happened. Stay close to Xander."

She promised she would, and shortly after, everyone left. Thick, gray clouds had rolled in, and thunder rumbled. As we headed inside, I knew I would do whatever it took to eliminate the fear and anxiety that clung to her.

24

XANDER

The scream had me out of bed with my gun in hand. Darkness was a silent presence in my room. No shadows separated or took form as a threat. In my gut, I knew it was Riley, and I cursed her stubborn desire to stay in the next cabin alone. A glance at the clock said it was predawn. With quick steps, I slipped from my house and into the night, making sure not to make a sound.

The air was cool, the moon a half crescent, lending a sliver of light that reflected off the rolling water to my right. Stars peppered the sky. No movement caught my attention.

After the body had washed up, my radar was on high alert. Both Jaxon and I agreed that Riley was at the center of this mess. The difference was that I was sure she was innocent.

I aimed my gun as I crept onto her porch then entered through the unlocked door. A soft whimper drew me to one of the bedrooms, and I crossed the family room to where she slept.

The shades were up, a breeze cooled the room from the open window, and the moon's silvery beam highlighted Riley as she tossed and turned in bed. I scanned the room before entering. With no threat detected, I secured my gun in my waistband.

A sob racked her chest, and she curled into a fetal position.

"Riley." I laid a hand on her shoulder, and she jackknifed upright. The sheet pooled around her waist, revealing a stretchy, pale T-shirt. With a push of the switch at the base of the bedside lamp, a soft glow encircled us.

Her wide eyes blinked. The moment her unfocused gaze cleared, she threw herself into my arms. I held her tightly, rubbing her back. It didn't take long before the tension in her body eased. Once she stopped shaking, I brushed a kiss across her forehead. In case it was a clue that would help find whomever was stalking her, I had to ask, "What were you dreaming about?"

"That night. The dreams returned when Charles and I fought and then the break-in made them worse. I see my parents lying there in a pool of blood. Their vacant stares… especially my mom's."

"Those images stay with us."

"My dad never wanted me. He would tell Mom she tricked him into marrying him."

"Then he was a fool, because you're worth everything." The thought of Riley, so young, blaming herself, and faced with one parent's abandonment, not to mention the abuse, left a bitter taste in my mouth.

She shifted in my arms. "I'm sure you deal with way worse when you have to go on missions."

"Death isn't easy. It haunts us. Shapes us."

Tears gathered and welled, but she blinked most of them away. "I'm all alone. Have been for so long."

I swept under her lashes, where wetness clung to the pad of my thumb. "You're not alone anymore. I'm here."

Neither of us moved. The rhythmic break of the waves was the only sound. Her hand cupped my cheek.

"Stay with me?"

I nodded then lay alongside her on the bed. She snuggled

close, and I traced circles on her arm with my thumb in a soothing motion. I wanted her but wouldn't push her. So much had happened, and the last thing I wanted was to take advantage.

"I was being stubborn, trying to prove that I could stay by myself after what happened to Charles. But the truth is, I want you, and I wasn't ready to fully admit how much." Her whisper-soft voice echoed what was in my mind. "I'm done fighting myself."

I shifted so we were face-to-face, and her gaze dropped to my mouth then lifted. When her pupils dilated, the last of my control evaporated, and I bent and brushed my lips across hers. Testing. It took all my strength to go slow, to let her tell me it was okay.

————

Riley

WHEN XANDER BROKE the drugging kiss, my dazed gaze clung to his features, taut with lust. He peeled away my T-shirt and stripped off my panties, his eyes dark and hungry. A shiver danced over my bare flesh as he dropped sensual kisses along the curve of my neck. I tilted my head to give him greater access.

I tugged at his offensive shorts, working to free him so there was nothing between us. His arms wound around me. *I've never wanted anyone as much as him.* He sealed his mouth over mine, and an electric current trailed in the wake of his touch. Sparks flew between us. His hands slid down my back and circled my waist before he lifted me on top of him.

The ebb and flow of the crashing waves couldn't compete with the roar of passion between us. He was long and hard between my thighs, and I rocked against him, thrilling in the low growl that rumbled deep in his chest. His fingers tangled in my hair and tugged my head back. I arched against him, and he trailed kisses lower. He took my nipple in his mouth and swirled his tongue around the tight peak, and I cried out. God, I wanted all of him.

"Please," I begged.

He released my hair and slipped his hand into the slickness between my thighs, and my body convulsed from the teasing caress. My hands clung to his shoulders, and I gasped when he increased the pressure.

I needed more. I tugged at the short hairs at the back of his head, urging him to give me release, to kiss me again. Pushing against his hand in frustration, I whimpered.

His deep, guttural voice ignited another surge of heat. "I want you, Riley."

My breath came in puffs, but I managed to whisper, "I want you too. Hurry." I needed him to fill me. He fumbled around with the nightstand drawer, and it sounded like he whispered a little prayer that his brother had left some behind. I heard the crinkle of a condom wrapper. Then his mouth slanted across mine, and I lost myself to his ministrations. So many sensations. When he teased my clit, spreading the slickness around the sensitive bud, my eyes about rolled back in my head. I couldn't take much more, and then he lined up against my entrance. I rocked against him, frantic in my need.

He thrust deeply, seating himself fully inside. I cried out as every nerve ending in my body was overstimulated in the best possible way. A fine sheen glistened over his chiseled chest in the moonlight, and my fingers danced over each ridge and valley.

His mouth captured mine again, his tongue caressing as he pulled out almost all the way, only to slide back in, over and over again. Stars exploded behind my eyelids, and heat blanketed every inch of my skin. The hard friction of his body drove me wild, and I tore my mouth from him as the orgasm seized my entire body.

A scream burst from my lips, and he swallowed it with his mouth, increasing his pace until he followed with his climax, just seconds after mine.

Secure in his arms and with our bodies joined, I never wanted to leave. He seemed content with our closeness, too, and we stayed like that while our breathing eased. His hand rubbed lazy circles around my back.

When the chilly air from the open window once again caused goose bumps to form on my exposed skin, Xander lifted me from him. Immediately, I felt the loss. He disposed of the condom then returned and wrapped me in his arms, situating us under the covers. My legs tangled with his, and my palm settled on his abdomen. I was exhausted, and it didn't take long for my satisfied body to hover on the verge of sleep.

I wanted to tell him that I loved him. In every way, Xander was what I wanted. I desperately hoped that everything would work out, and I could keep him.

———

VISIONS of what Xander did to me last night invaded my mind, and I swept my hair into a messy bun as heat infused my flushed skin. After waking me from the dream and making love, he'd spent the night. I'd awoken halfway sprawled across his chest, with our legs tangled together. I nibbled on my lower lip. Lying in his arms had been comforting and natural, and we'd stayed in bed, talking.

He'd reassured me again that I wasn't alone, and for the first time, that emptiness inside me wasn't a gaping hole. It shrank to a dull ache. In time, if things continued to progress and go well between us, I thought it might go away. He made me feel safe, happy, and loved.

With a sigh, I opened my laptop and stared at a blank Word document. I needed to write a cover letter then paste it into an email to the New York gallery.

Xander had gone for a swim, and I found myself watching his powerful strokes instead of working. With a resigned sigh, I closed the laptop and set it next to the book. My fingers brushed the raised silver spiderweb design on the cover, and a sense of unease settled in my gut. I needed to talk to Xander about the similarities in some scenes and see what he thought.

The towel on the chair next to me was dry, so I grabbed that, sunglasses, and *The Spider's Prey* then went to wait for him to finish his laps. Once I had the towel spread out, I sat cross-legged and thumbed through the book, finding the scene where the story's protagonist poisons her husband.

Minutes later, Xander emerged from the ocean with water clinging to all the places I would like to touch. The thought of running my hands over every inch of him sent a wave of heat to my core. The sexy grin that curved his lips let me know he knew what I was thinking.

It wasn't the time. I couldn't put off showing him the scene. As far as I knew, there weren't any leads on Charles's death. The only clues pointed to me, and I was aware that Xander was the reason I wasn't behind bars.

My stomach swirled with a deadly combination of desire and dread for my future. *Will we have one? Or is mine already decided?* My family history was bleak, and I wanted—no, needed—to break the pattern. That meant I had to consider every possible clue, bring them forward, and be an active participant in clearing my name of Charles's death if the blood on my apartment door was found to be his. I couldn't just lean on Xander's capable shoulders, no matter how appealing that was.

After he took a seat next to me on the extra towel, I picked up the hardcover and opened it to the start of the scene. "This is weird, but I swear this scene is similar to what's happened with

Charles and me." I tapped the page. "Check it out. Tell me I'm crazy."

Heat radiated off his body and into mine as we sat side by side. Our fingers brushed as he pulled the book onto his lap, and I shivered from the contact.

"What am I looking for?"

"Here,"—I pointed to the start of the paragraph—"where the male lead is poisoned."

I couldn't shake the unease that what had happened to Charles and me was the product of a copycat killer.

Xander bent his head as he read where I'd indicated. With my arms looped around my bent legs, I dug my heels into the sand.

When he reached the end of the scene and met my gaze with a seriousness that gave me pause, my worry escalated tenfold.

"This is weird, but it's probably nothing. Try not to worry about it."

"There's another part." I took the book back, flipping through the pages until I found what I was looking for. "Right here, the wife hits the, ah, mistress"—I couldn't stop the cringe even if I wanted to—"with a baseball bat."

I handed the book over when he tugged on the corner, watching the frown deepen as he skimmed it.

"This isn't what happened to you, though. It's different enough." He winked then tapped the tip of my nose. "Maybe reading a thriller isn't the best thing, considering all that's happened?"

"God, that's so true." I rolled my eyes so hard I almost listed to the side. "I'm feeling a little too dramatic." With a thump, I closed the book and set it aside. I flashed him a smile. Even though he'd shown concern at the one scene, I was glad he wasn't overly worried. "Thanks. I'm probably overthinking this." I was feeling much better, and a thrill shot through me from our close proximity.

"I think we need to do something to take your mind off things." His wolfish grin made me laugh.

"Surfing?" I suggested, knowing it wasn't where his thoughts were focused but wanting to work off some of the stress I was experiencing. Tonight, we would explore his ideas, and for the first time in a long while, I couldn't wait for darkness to fall.

25

RILEY

The delicious smell of bacon pulled me from a deep sleep Thursday morning, and I patted Xander's spot with my hand. The indent was still there from where his head had rested. A grin stretched my mouth wide, and I buried my face in his pillow, inhaling his intoxicating scent.

When we were done on the beach, Xander had pulled me close and whispered what he wanted to do to me. Like the Pied Piper, I'd willingly followed. We were up most of the night, and I was deliciously relaxed.

I swung my legs over the side of the bed then padded to the master bathroom. It didn't take long to brush my teeth and take a quick shower. I put on a bathing suit and a cover-up because I wanted to work outside rather than be cooped up in a room.

At the entrance to the kitchen, I paused. Xander was at the stovetop, flipping bacon. With each motion of the spatula, muscles rippled across his broad back. There were a few scars, including the recent one from the gunshot wound. I'd traced them last night, brushing kisses over every mark then swirling my tongue over that sexy-as-hell tattoo he had on his bicep. Heat pooled in my core, and I wanted him again. It was that simple. All I had to do was look at him, hear the deep timbre of his voice, or feel the electric current of his touch, and I was a needy mess.

I must have made a noise, because he turned, wearing that grin I loved. With an internal shake to loosen the thrall of lust, I crossed to the coffee machine. "Want a cup?"

"Sure, love." He served eggs and bacon onto two plates. "Do you want to go for a run on the beach after I swim a few miles?"

He rounded the peninsula, where I was already seated with my breakfast and steaming hot coffee. Before he sat next to me, he cupped the back of my neck and brushed his lips across mine. I wanted more, but we both had things to get done, so I settled instead for the promise of that night.

We chatted as we ate, the conversation effortless and fun. Even being silent together was companionable—I just liked being with him. It felt right.

About an hour later, Xander went for his swim while I gathered what I needed to work on and settled on the beach, this time in a chair.

It was in the quiet moments like those that Charles's death invaded my mind. I blinked back tears and rubbed at my chest. I had to keep my mind off what had happened, or I would fall victim to hours of sobbing. I might have been done with him, but he didn't have to die.

I'd decided to occupy myself with the little bit of work I had to do. The laptop booted up, and then I stared at a blank screen. *Why is this so intimidating?* It was just a cover letter and shouldn't have been so hard. I clicked around until I pulled up an email from a few years ago that I'd sent to my agent for one of the Chicago galleries. This would be easier. With a few changes, it was ready to go. I attached the pictures then used my phone's hot spot to send everything off.

Close to sunset, I decided to go for a quick run. Xander had been working in one of the houses for a couple of hours, allowing me to relax. With the only thing I had to do finished, I put my laptop in the sleeve and then in my beach bag to protect it from the sand. A missed call from Ava showed on my phone, but she hadn't left a message. I texted, feeling guilty that I hadn't told her about everything that had happened, but I didn't want to alarm her while she was working. Not even two seconds later, my phone rang, and her name flashed across the screen.

"Hey! I'm so glad you called. I'm sorry I missed you earlier."

"Hi back." Ava's voice carried a smile, and I could picture her grinning. "Is that the ocean I'm hearing? Are you at the beach?"

"Yeah." I nibbled on my bottom lip. "I'm with Xander."

"Good for you. I'm glad you're moving on from the professor." She laughed. "From the sound of your voice, things are good?"

Shit. I blinked back tears then forced a steadiness I didn't quite feel into my voice. "Between Xander and me, yes. But there's been some pretty bad stuff that's happened, so I'm on his island with him."

Silence met my ear from the other end, and my stomach tightened.

I was going to have to tell her. "Ava?"

"I'm here." She sounded tense and worried. "What's going on? Do I need to fly you out to me? I can stay longer, and we can spend the extra days shopping."

My heart melted. "Thanks, Aves, but I'm okay for now. Finish up with work, and I'll catch up when you get back next week."

"I'm coming back Sunday, but if you don't tell me right now what happened, I'll jump on the next flight and come to you."

She was tenacious, and there would be no avoiding telling her. "To start with, my apartment was broken into again."

"Were you there?"

"No, thankfully." I blew out a breath and got ready for her reaction. "But there was blood on the door and a knife. We don't know where that came from yet, but obviously, I can't live there anymore. Xander came to the rescue."

"That's scary as hell. I'm just glad he was there for you. Were there prints on the knife? Do you know who's behind this?"

"The only prints were mine. It was one of my kitchen knives."

"Did you think the professor's behind it?"

"It crossed my mind until two days ago, when his body washed up on a reef here."

"What?!" There was a sound like she'd dropped the phone, but then she was back on the line. "I don't understand. Is the professor dead? As in drowned?"

"Yes." Tears filled my eyes at the thought. I'd made my peace with letting our relationship go, but that didn't mean I'd stopped caring for him completely.

"I'm so sorry, Riles. Maybe you shouldn't stay there. So much has happened. Fly out to me in California. A change of scenery might be best."

But I couldn't. Not with the ongoing investigation. I rolled onto my stomach on the towel. I caught a glimpse of Xander on the roof of the house he was working on from my new view. His shoulders glistened and flexed as he nailed the new material in place. My stomach clenched, and my heart pounded. I had my answer. "It would be the best thing to do, but there's Xander."

"Hotness versus shopping. I see your dilemma."

"Yeah, I can't seem to tear myself away from him. A part of me wishes I'd met Xander first. It's different with him. Intense. If I'd never gotten involved with Charles, maybe he would still be alive."

"You can't think like that. Oh God—I wonder how his wife took the news."

The pleasant burn from watching Xander extinguished with that comment, replaced by ice in my veins. "I don't know. I'm not going to go anywhere near her. I can't imagine how she's doing. Do you know that he told me he demanded a divorce? Like I would take him back after what he did to another woman. It was crazy."

"That poor woman." Ava huffed. "Well, I'm sure she's happily spending his money now."

"I guess there's that." I rubbed my forehead, debating whether or not to tell Ava the rest.

"Is something else wrong? You went silent over there, and I swear I can hear your mind spinning."

"I'm worried that the police think I'm a suspect. The blood that was on my door was human."

"What does that mean?"

"I have no idea, but it's concerning."

"I can't imagine they would think you're to blame. Go be with your guy, and don't let this get to you. It'll all work out."

I wasn't so sure. "Thanks, Aves."

"I've got to run, but please call me if you need me, or when you find out anything more."

After we disconnected, I tried to let the sense of impending disaster go, but it was pointless. For some reason, death stalked me, and I worried about what could be next.

———

Xander

CLOUDS FILTERED THROUGH THE SKY, giving momentary breaks from the intense heat of the sun's rays while I made repairs to Tyler's roof. Sweat trickled down my forehead. I wiped it away with the back of my hand before it ran into my eyes.

I was headed down the ladder for a drink of water when my

phone rang. I crossed to where I'd left it on the partially finished deck then answered after Jaxon's name flashed across the screen.

"Any news?" My gaze strayed to Riley, who was lying on her stomach and talking on the phone. I could tell he was at work by the clinking sound of handcuffs and the distant whine of a siren leaving the station.

"Not anything good."

That got my attention. "Tell me."

"I looked into the hospital report when you told me about how Riley took Charles to the ER for a possible heart attack, the night she broke up with him."

"And?"

"Higher than normal levels of nitroglycerin were found in his blood. When questioned at the hospital, he denied taking any heart medications that would have explained the substance's presence. I confirmed from his medical records that it wasn't prescribed, either."

"I fail to understand why that's important. He could've had chest pains, and a friend gave it to him."

"Here's where it gets interesting," Jaxon explained, his voice as hushed as it could be amidst the noise of a police station. "If mixed with alcohol, it causes abnormal heart rhythms and fainting. There's a chance she poisoned him. She'd told the nurse when she first got there that he'd had some wine at her house. When Nolan gets wind of this information—and we just got it so that'll be soon—he'll roll with it, using the theory that she tried to kill him before his actual death and that neither incidents were accidental."

Something about what he'd told me struck a chord, and my mind raced to make the connection.

"Another thing—and this is why Nolan hasn't seen the tox report yet. A bodiless foot and shoe were found."

"Was it Charles's?"

"No. A woman's. I don't have any other information than that."

There had to be a connection there. I could hear someone yell for Jaxon and knew he would have to go.

"We should have the results back from forensics and the coroner's office shortly, which will also tell us if the blood found on Riley's apartment door is a match for Charles. Just, be careful."

"That goes without saying." I didn't tell him, but I was grateful Jaxon was involved in this mess.

"You're sure about her?"

"She's the one." That's all I needed to say to him. I ground my teeth as the similarities about what Jax had told me about Charles's hospital results connected to the scene in the book Riley had shown me.

"Hell, Xan, I'm glad to hear that, but this is a shit show."

"There's more." I told him about the book Riley was reading and how she thought maybe there was a connection between Charles and the author.

"What, like a girlfriend scorned?"

I had no idea. "Not sure. It's just a theory." I gave him the name of the author. "Can you look into it?"

"Wouldn't hurt."

"What about the wife? Riley said Charles was filing for divorce the last time she saw him."

"She has an alibi. I've got to warn you that we've got nothing else to clear Riley if the blood on her door was his. There's something else. The knife found on the door didn't match the cuts on Charles's foot, but it also didn't look exactly like a shark."

"What are you thinking?"

"The barista the other coffee bar whose foot was found severed from her body. It was assumed a shark was the cause. No foul play was suspected."

"But you found something."

"Yes. Both were severed at the same spot above the ankle, and the skin looks like shark teeth did the deed. But there are inconsistencies which lead us to believe it was caused by a shark-toothed weapon."

Dammit. I'd seen those in a museum. Rows of razor-sharp sharks' teeth were fitted into wooden swords. "So you're looking for another weapon?"

"You got it," Jaxon replied. "Nothing turned up in Riley's apartment, but I need you to go through her things."

"I was with her the whole time she packed. There is no knife."

"Just be sure, Xan. What if she's a killer?"

"She's not," I countered. I knew my brother meant well, but I was starting to get angry. "Not that she's anything like what you're worried about, but I can handle myself just fine."

"Not when your heart is involved."

26

XANDER

The screen door slammed behind me as I entered my house to find Riley sitting at the kitchen table with her laptop open to a breathtaking picture of a lookout point on Oahu.

She didn't notice me until I stood at her side. "That's beautiful. Did you take it?"

"Yes, but there's something here that I hadn't noticed at first. Because of that, I didn't include it in my thesis."

"Why? I can't see anything wrong."

"I missed it the first time, but check this out." Quizzical eyes met mine before she focused back on the picture. "Here." She tapped a fingernail not far from the rock outcropping along the coastline. "This is a face. Super hard to see, but magnify it, and the features are partially visible between the rocks."

With a few clicks, she enhanced the image so that I was looking at a small cove within the cliff. I braced myself on her chair and the table, leaning over her to see what she was doing.

Goddamn. She was right. It was blurry and partially hidden until she made a few adjustments.

My thoughts flew to our last mission. *What if that's what we missed? If there was someone else there in the jungle that the infrared imaging hadn't captured?* I needed to get to the base and take another look at the pictures from the Black Hawk. It was a long shot but well worth a second look.

I grinned at her. She didn't know it, but she'd given me an idea that could potentially reveal information that we'd overlooked. I gave her long hair a gentle tug and pressed a kiss to her lips. "It's gorgeous, even with the photobomb. In fact, that makes it more interesting."

She grinned. "Thanks."

Riley and her picture had diverted my attention, which wasn't uncommon or unwanted—she frequently distracted me. There was news I had to tell her from Jaxon, and I would deliver it as soon as I spoke with Ty. I picked up the sandwich she'd made for me and inhaled it. By the time she finished, the food had turned to lead in my stomach. I thanked her for the sandwich, told her I had to make a call, and stepped outside. As soon as I was clear of hearing distance, I hit Tyler's contact to call him. I got to the point as soon as he answered.

"Where are you?" I asked. I knew I had to be careful. If there was a mole, as we'd expected, then we had to be smart. What I hoped was that we could find something in the pictures that would point us in a new direction.

"I'm on base."

"Go somewhere secure."

There was a sound of a door closing, then the background noise went silent. "What's going on?"

"We need to recheck the Black Hawk's images. What if we missed something, and it's not cartel who hit us?"

We wrapped up our conversation, and my thoughts shifted back to Riley. Stowing my phone in my pocket, I went inside and gathered her in my arms. I had to tell her what Jaxon relayed to me. "I talked to my brother. That night Charles was taken to the hospital, they found nitroglycerin in his blood. The amount caused a reaction with the wine he drank."

She jerked in my arms, lifted her head from my chest, and leaned back, her eyes wide with shock. "They think it was me, don't they? Oh God, the book—"

I ran my hand along her back in a soothing motion. "Jaxon is looking into the author. They have another lead, so the connection is good."

"What if the author is Melanie?" She worried her lip for a moment. "She missed a shift, and Jeff and Chloe were worried about her. They weren't able to reach her. She told me she's an author and has published under a pen name."

"Why do you think those things are related?"

"Because she dated Charles and was extremely jealous. What if she was like the wife in the book, who posed as a student to find out about the women her husband cheated with?"

She had a point. I pulled my phone from my pocket. After pressing Jaxson's contact info again, I waited for him to pick up. Several rings later, it went to voicemail, where I left him a detailed message about Melanie. "He'll check her out, too, when he gets the message."

"All right." A small smile eased some of the tension on her face. "Thanks."

"It'll be okay." I drew her to me, wishing I could erase her worry. "I'm with you every step of the way."

———

Riley

THERE WAS a slight chill to the air—Xander had left the door to the cabin open to allow the strengthening breeze in. Electricity charged the air, and through the screen door, I could see thick clouds headed our way. After a while, I was over the shock of learning the cause of Charles's symptoms and the parallel to the book, so Xander was comfortable leaving me for an hour to finish the roof. If he didn't finish, it would leak when it rained later that night—we were due for another storm.

I stayed inside, cleaning up our lunch. When that was done, I wanted to change out of my bathing suit. So I went next door, where I'd spent the first night on the island. He'd told me to move my clothes in with his, but I hadn't yet. It was time.

It was hard to believe it was Friday, only two days from graduation, where all would feel Charles's absence. I knew it was the right decision not to go. There would be too much speculation if the connection between us was discovered.

As it was, news of his death had gone out in an email from the university to the students, minus key details. In a slow blink, I shoved the image of Charles's lifeless body away and focused on why I was in the adjacent house to Xanders.

I'd left my book on the lanai and grabbed it as I moved through the house to toss it in my bag with everything else. I set the bag on the peninsula then straightened up the kitchen and wiped the counters. With the dishes put away, nothing looked out of place.

Muted sunlight filtered through the open window, and a cooling breeze forecasted the approaching stormy weather. The palm tree fronds that surrounded the sides and back of the house rustled in the wind, and I hoped Xander would be done soon—I was still uneasy and wanted to talk to him again about the scenes in the novel and play devil's advocate about Mel fitting the profile. I padded into the bedroom to finish gathering my things but stopped short.

My clothes were strewn about, with some on the floor and the rest on the bed. My heart slammed against my chest. I hadn't done that, and I was fairly certain that Xander hadn't either, but he was the only other person on the island. I frowned as I picked everything up. It was weird, but I couldn't figure out what other reason there was for the mess.

Once I'd changed into a T-shirt and shorts and all my stuff was back in the bag, I made the bed and sat down, the picture I'd helped Xander enhance filling my head. *What if I'm missing something too?* I pulled the book into my lap and stared at the author's picture. *Could this be Melanie?* My computer was still on Xander's kitchen table, so I couldn't upload a digital image and do any editing to see if there was something familiar. I had to rely on my vision.

Inch by inch, I went over the details. The shape of her face, the Gucci oversized sunglasses—oh my God, I knew who had a pair exactly like them, with the same minuscule scratch on the edge of the right lens.

It couldn't have been her. My hand shook, and my eyes misted, the picture blurring in front of me. I couldn't handle another betrayal. There had to be some other explanation.

I must have sat on the edge of the bed, staring blindly out the window, for a half hour, maybe longer. A part of me had already accepted that she had abandoned me in the worst possible way, just like my father.

With a pen from my purse, I circled the scratch on the author's photo then jumped to my feet when the door closed behind me. The book tumbled to the floor, and I whirled around to find Ava there. "What are you doing here?"

She no longer wore her signature bun—her blond hair was down, and she had on the same sunglasses from the author picture.

"It's you, isn't it?"

She laughed, and chills erupted along my arms. "I didn't think you'd figure it out. What gave me away?" She tugged on a strand of hair. "This?"

"Yep." I wasn't going to tell her. I wanted to leave the clue I'd circled in case Xander found the picture. Not that he would know Ava had the same frames, but I'd scribbled her name above the sunglasses with a question mark. There was no doubt in my mind that he would share that information with Jaxon, and they would both look for me—if she didn't kill me first. "What I don't understand is why."

"Why what?" She pulled a gun from her oversized bag and pointed it at me. "Why did Charles have to die? Why did I leave you for last?"

"You're my friend." I choked on the last word, taking several deep breaths to regain some degree of calm.

"Oh, sweetheart. Don't you know how far a woman scorned will go?"

"You were his girlfriend?" He'd had many from what I'd learned, so it wasn't a stretch. I'd entertained the idea that the author was Mel, but obviously, C. Marx was Ava's pen name. I wondered if Charles's wife had known about Ava's obsession.

A bitter laugh ripped from her mouth. "We're not doing this here. Get up."

I shook my head, standing my ground. "I'm not going anywhere with you."

She lunged, and I glimpsed the gun before she pistol-whipped the side of my head.

I couldn't move. My temple throbbed, pain radiating outward. She had the gun fisted in her hand, pointed directly at me.

"You'll be fine. Get up."

On shaky legs, I stood. She pulled some duct tape from her pocket and put a small strip over my mouth.

"This is just until we're out of hearing distance. Can't keep it on too long, or it will leave marks." With the gun, she motioned for me to go.

The hard barrel of the weapon pressed against my side. She grabbed my arm and headed out of the house, moving quickly to the side where Xander was not. The sky had darkened, the wind gained strength, and the clouds were thick and angry.

Ava peeked around the corner to see if Xander was looking while I berated myself for not attacking her first. Shock had made me an easy target. First, finding out that she was the author of the book I was reading—not Mel. There were similarities I couldn't ignore in several of the scenes. The sunglasses. Then the unexpected attack. The medication found in Charles's blood. It was a lot. I couldn't dwell on it. When we were clear, she tore the tape from my mouth, making my eyes water.

There would be a time when she didn't have the gun wedged against my skin. When I found a break, I would go for it. I just had to stay vigilant and block the pain in my head.

Because if I didn't, she was sure to kill me, and it didn't seem as if it was her first time.

27

RILEY

Ava poked me in the back with the gun, urging me to hurry. The howling wind tangled my hair around my face, making it difficult to see where to walk through the flourishing vegetation on Xander's island. Fat drops of rain slipped through the trees, and we had to pick our way through plants and fallen coconuts. Mangos, plantains, and an overabundance of ferns meant there was no navigable path.

The storm wouldn't last long. They rarely did because of the trade winds.

A portion of the terrain rose at a fairly steep angle, covered with dense trees and bushes. Xander had told me a part of the island was a rocky cliff. Ava dragged me around the base of it and away from the houses. She must have set up a way off the island on the other side.

The ache in my temple increased with each step, and a small trickle of blood ran along the side of my hairline. Through the panic and physical discomfort, I racked my brain for ways to get away from her. *Keep her talking.* Given the gun, I couldn't see an easy way to overpower her. A wave of dizziness swept through me, and I stumbled and went down on one knee.

"Get up," Ava said with a growl. Rain dotted her face, and she hauled me to my feet.

I pulled away from her grip and half pivoted to try to make a break for it. Pain exploded through my back, and I whimpered. She'd jammed the barrel of the gun into my spine.

"Don't even think about it. I'll shoot you here if I have to."

Damn it. "Why are you doing this?"

"No more talking." She dragged me forward.

I had to make it difficult for her. With my feet feeling like lead, I stumbled several more times. Under the shade of the trees, we were spared from the heavy rainfall, but the little that slipped through softened the ground.

We trudged through the underbrush. I stomped around, dragging my feet as much as possible, forcing her to dig her heels in too. There would be a trail to find me.

"I think you gave me a concussion. I'm dizzy and can't walk straight." I couldn't help the rising hysteria from infusing my voice.

She snorted. "That's the least of your worries. Hurry up." She tugged harder. "We're almost there."

Shit. I let my legs go weak and slid onto my side on the damp ground, going down on a fern, purposely flattening it while dragging the bloodied side of my head over as many of the plants nearby as I could under the guise of regaining my feet.

"Stay on your goddamn feet!" Ava shouted between clenched teeth, her face taut in anger. Blond hair tangled around her head, forcing the glare she shot me to play hide and seek between the shifting strands. I shivered—not from cold but from the borderline-insane expression in her empty eyes.

The trees parted ahead to reveal a splash of choppy blue-gray water against an angry sky. I was running out of time. Not only that, but I had no idea when Xander would start looking for me or if he would be in time—I only knew that he would.

I had to stall.

"I don't understand why you're doing this. You know I broke up with Charles. I wasn't competition."

"Oh, honey. As if." Ava's deranged laugh cut through the thunder's low rumble. "None of Charles's extracurricular girls were a threat or even difficult to handle."

"Then why? What was he to you?"

Pain shot through my skull as she grabbed a chunk of my hair and yanked.

"Ow!" I clutched my head in agony. Spots swam in my vision. I gasped, trying to breathe through the misery.

"I'm his *wife*."

"What?" Her words sliced though my pain. We were facing each other. Her fury dilated her pupils to pinpricks and leached all color from her lips. "That can't be. I saw a picture of his wife, and you look nothing like her. And your name is different." *Is she delusional too?* "His wife's last name is Wright."

"Yeah, Chava Wright. Ava is short for Chava, and I don't use my married name for publishing under either genre. And appearances are easy to change. All it takes is a little contouring, colored contacts, and a wig."

Holy shit. She wrote fiction as C. Marx, and for nonfiction, she was Ava Murphy. "Charles worked with you on some of the academic stuff."

"He was such a baby about that. As if I could highlight his name anywhere in association to mine. I wasn't stupid. What if one of you found out?" She shoved me forward so I would resume walking. "It was bad enough that I liked you."

"Then why do this?"

"You knew too much, and then you started to read my book."

"You didn't want me to?"

We'd cleared the trees and were on the beach. There was a rowboat with a motor, docked in the sand with the engine pulled up so it wouldn't get ruined.

"No, you ordering a copy wasn't in the plan. It'd just been

released, and I was looking forward to rereading it. You were so nosey that I had to go with being a fan, which is funny because I am."

"Melanie read it too. If you didn't want me to read it, why not say it sucked?"

"Eh, I sort of did want you to. It's damn good. You even replayed a few of those scenes."

"I didn't fall down any stairs."

"No. But I did hit you with a weighted purse when you rounded the corner."

I sucked in air. Of course that had been her. It made sense. She had done all of it. "Where did you go? I never even saw you."

"I ducked into the store next door and slipped out the back. I knew where the cameras were. I was careful. You weren't paying attention. It was easy."

"And the hospital visit? Did you want me to find out about Charles having a wife?"

Laughter rose over the roar of the frothing waves. "That was a kindness. I liked you, which was something I hadn't expected. I wanted to forgive you." Ava's blue eyes were wild, and her mouth was pinched tight with barely restrained fury. "When you found out about his wife, you did the right thing. Turned him away. Felt remorse. It wasn't quite enough for me, but I was willing to release you from the damage of dating a married man."

"What about Mel? You had to know she was seeing Charles."

Ava grimaced. "She was a plaything for him and not really worth my time. I knew he didn't think much of her. Besides, she was the perfect scapegoat for anything I planned to do. It was well-known that she was obsessed with him. But in the end, I took care of her too."

The pieces fell into place, and tremors wracked my body.

She motioned for me to help her shove the boat off the sand

and into the water. When we were both knee-deep, she pointed the gun at me again, and I climbed in. Waves crashed against us, and we rocked back onto the bank. "Get out." With one hand on the side of the boat, she pointed the weapon straight at me. "Push us out. And if you think to try to swim away, I can just as easily shoot you from here." She shrugged. "Either way, here or out there, you'll die."

I got us out farther, and she flipped the engine into the water then started it. "Get in."

It was a miracle that I didn't capsize us. I thought about it, but she had a bead on me, and that wouldn't have changed. There wouldn't have been enough time to swim under before she shot me, most likely in the head.

The storm's howling wind and rain picked up. With the waves gaining in height and strength, she wouldn't be able to stay out long. "Where are you taking us?"

"Not far."

I gripped the side of the boat with both hands, hanging on for all I was worth as she hurtled us through the choppy water. The small vessel crashed with a thump into each wave. It took time. The current was strong, and I worried that if I dived in, I wouldn't be able to swim back. But the waves were high enough that she couldn't shoot with a steady aim.

I shifted closer to the edge, but she lifted the gun and pointed it directly at my chest. "Don't do it. I'll shoot you before you hit the water."

Ava's back was to the shoreline, and I faced her. She cut the engine and reached under one of the metal seats. A dark and stained duffel bag appeared in her hand. I didn't want to think about what had caused the marks. Again, I glanced at the island, hoping to see Xander. I thought I saw a head appear between the waves, but after I stared at the general area for a while, I realized I was wrong.

Ava's hand was on the zipper, and I freaked. I had an idea of what she had in there. The boat rocked, causing my stomach to roll even more.

"We'll hang here for a little while," Ava said with an eerie calmness. "I need time to cut your foot off."

"Why would you do that?" Panic was ping-ponging to the point where my voice was high and shrill, and tremors shook my limbs.

She paused again. "It's what I do. I gave you a hint when we first met."

"Oh God, the other coffee house. The barista." *And Charles. Probably Mel too.*

"Yep. Charles had a thing for waitresses of all sorts. Anyone who would serve him was a huge turn-on. Men." She shook her head.

She must have thought I would commiserate, but all I could do was stare at her in horror while frantically wracking my brain for anything to keep her talking. "Why the foot?"

"I read about it happening somewhere else and thought that was a good way to muddy the waters. When the foot washed up, it would appear as if a shark ate the rest of the person." She shrugged again. "I liked it. Whoever started it had a great idea. And whatever is left of the body will wash up."

She was twisted. The wind picked up, and the boat rocked dangerously from side to side. "Why did you kill Charles?"

Her cold, dead eyes met mine. "He filed for divorce. It was unacceptable, unimaginable, and I couldn't let you live. You ruined everything. Until you, we had an ironclad promise to each other, one that we would keep. He was mine until death."

"You won't get away with this. The police will figure it out and find you."

She laughed, and the twisted sound mingled with the howling wind in an eerie symphony. "No one will find me. I have a contingency plan. Bank accounts and residency were established years ago. I'll move away and become my fictional name."

———

Xander

THE SKY DARKENED, and the wind flung bits of leaves and pelting sand around. With the repair completed, I was done for the day —and just in time, as rain peppered the metal roofing. I climbed down the ladder, picked up all my tools, then locked them in Tyler's house for the next project.

After a quick scan of the beach and lanais with no sign of Riley, I headed for my house. She'd probably gone inside to escape the storm that was quickly arriving. The screen door slammed behind me, and with a shove, I opened the door between the porch and house. "Riley?"

There was no answering reply. I did a walk-through then went back out to look in the house we'd slept in the first night, where I figured she was gathering all her stuff. Once inside, I found her bag but no Riley. My instincts spiked. Something had to have happened. That was when I saw a tiny speck of something on the wood floor. I dabbed at the still-wet spot then lifted my finger to get a better look. It was blood.

I whirled around and searched the house as I yanked my cell phone from my pocket, called Jaxon, and cursed until he picked up. "She's gone."

"Riley? Shit, I was about to call you. The author of that book was Charles's wife."

"I'm going after them. There's a drop of blood on the floor. Get over here fast." I thought of Charles's body and how we'd found him. "Alert the Coast Guard."

I didn't hear what else he had to say. I'd already disconnected and shoved the phone back into my pocket. We kept guns in all the houses. I located one and secured it into the back of my jeans, palming a knife from the kitchen as I passed through.

My resolve hardened to get her back, and I scanned the waters, hunting for any sign of Riley. Then I circled the house, looking for prints. There was a smear of blood on the edge of the back door. Part of a fern lay twisted, as if someone had ground their foot on the leaves. *Thank you, Riley.* As quickly as I could, I sprinted through the woods, banking hard at the sight of a footprint just as the terrain sloped upward. She'd left clues along the way. One pair of prints was sloppy, digging into the earth, with what appeared to be a knee print. The other set went deeper in at those spots, too, but little was disturbed otherwise.

They were headed to the leeward side of the island. There would be a boat there, and given the storm, we wouldn't have heard it approach. The wind sailed through the trees, and the forest came alive. Leaves danced and bobbed, and one place where the mud was heavily displaced revealed smears of blood on nearby leaves. Urgency nipped at my heels, and fear for Riley drove me to hurry.

From the edge of the trees, I skidded to a stop. A small boat listed precariously amidst the rolling waves. Triangular waves rocked the boat as they fed under and pushed it toward the shore. I squinted to bring them into focus while redialing Jaxon. There were two women in the vessel, Riley and some blonde. *I'm not too late.*

I told Jaxon where we were. Disconnecting, I dropped my phone then peeled off my jeans and shoes. The blonde's back was to the shore. It took a second to judge the distance to know I couldn't get a clean shot. With the gun in my hand and my knife clamped between my teeth, I sprinted to the water, diving under as soon as I was deep enough.

The Coast Guard wouldn't get there in time. I had to. The undertow worked against me as I swam beneath the water, only coming up for air when necessary. Fear and guilt warred inside me, spurring me to swim faster. I'd brought her onto the island to keep her safe, and then this happened. Holding my breath and fighting against the ocean wasn't the problem. It was the blind fear about what that woman was doing to Riley. Charles had been missing a foot. It was possible the other murders with bodies or only feet washing up could be pinned on the blonde.

I broke the surface. Not long and I would reach the boat. I ducked back under. If the blonde noticed and spotted me, I would lose the element of surprise.

The usually clear water was murky with disturbed sand and churning undertow. The bottom of the boat was in sight. I had one chance. Diving deeper, I positioned myself underneath it before angling toward the side to remain undetected. My hand lightly brushed the underside. I switched the knife from my mouth to my free hand. With powerful kicks, I launched upward to break the surface on the side where I estimated the blonde would be. My hand gripped the top of the boat, and I pulled myself up, bursting free and rising to the side.

The woman turned and saw me. An outraged shriek competed with the thunder, and the barrel of her gun swung toward me. I stabbed the knife into her arm. She screamed. Blood welled around the wound. Riley flung her hands at the blonde's wrist, throwing the gun's trajectory off course. I grabbed the woman and yanked her toward me. The expelled round missed both of us. Keeping a tight grip on her, I released the boat, sucked in air, and dragged her over and under. Beneath the water, I twisted her gun-wielding hand until she released it.

Light hair floated in a cloud around her head, obscuring her face. Didn't matter. My elbow clipped her hard in the head. Her body went limp. I slipped my arm around her and held her against me then swam close to the boat.

We broke the surface. I had the blonde supported so that her head was above water as I shouted to Riley over the sound of the thunder and cresting waves, "Are you all right?"

"Yes!" Riley leaned over the edge, tears on her cheeks mingling with the rain. "How do I get you in here?"

"I got this, just hold on." I tossed the unconscious woman into the boat. Riley held onto the side of the boat as it rocked in the choppy water. I needed to take her in my arms and feel for myself that she was truly alive.

A small duffel bag was opened at her feet, and I caught a glimpse of the shark-tooth machete. I hauled myself into the boat, thanking every power that be that I was able to get to her in time. Riley launched herself into my arms, and I squeezed her tightly.

Her heart pounded against my chest, and I breathed her in. *She's safe.*

Holding her wasn't enough. I'd almost lost her. I had to feel more of her, touch her. I buried my hands in her hair. She whimpered in anticipation as I tilted her head back, bent, and caressed her lips, savoring her softness and her quick intake of breath. What started slow and soft became demanding with every brush of our tongues. She pressed against me, her touch warm and welcoming, a promise of much more. I deepened our passionate kiss, moaning at how good she tasted, how right she felt in my arms.

When we broke apart, I rested my forehead against hers while our breaths mingled in labored puffs. I knew that I would never be able to let her go.

I cupped her face, holding her gently. Her hair danced on the wind, and I looped it around my hand. We were one with the sea, rocking with the swells. Help was on the way.

Her fingers curled against me, and I fought the urge to kiss her again, but there were things I had to say. "I never thought I would find you. When I heard your voice and saw you that day when you were working at the Coffee Hut, I knew you were the one. We began as friends, but I wanted you always. I love you, Riley."

Lightning painted the sky, highlighting the emotion that blazed in her eyes. Her fingers traced the side of my face then slipped behind my neck.

I would follow her to hell and back to hold her in my arms—to have her be mine.

"Xander, you've changed my life and filled what was missing inside of me. I love you too." Tears leaked from her joy-filled eyes.

Off in the distance, we heard the Coast Guard approach. Soon, they would take over with Riley's attacker.

I sealed our promise to one another with a drugging kiss. She was my partner, my lover, my everything.

The Coast Guard lined up beside the boat we were in, and I pulled Riley against my side. Jaxon and one of the men boarded, and I met my brother's concerned gaze.

We switched boats and were given blankets. While they secured Ava and brought her stash of weapons onboard, Jaxon met my gaze with a fierce frown. He squatted down to eye level with Riley and gave her shoulder a squeeze. "I can take a brief statement from you now, and we'll drop you and Xander off before we book Chava."

Riley and I summed up the events that lead to Chava, or Ava, being subdued, including the part where she'd confessed to Riley about killing Mel. It didn't take long before we were dropped off at the shore by the cabins. Once we were inside, I would show her just how much I loved her.

28

XANDER

Sun streamed through the windows with the promise of a beautiful day. Riley and I sat on the screened patio with coffee and bacon-and-cheese soufflés. I had to attend a meeting at Pearl Harbor, and until I had to leave, I wanted to spend every moment I could with her. Waking that morning with Riley in my arms was an experience I would never tire of.

She had her legs tucked under her, and her gaze caught mine over the rim of her coffee. A deep sadness rimmed the softer emotions in her pretty eyes, and I wished I could have stopped Ava before she'd ever gotten to the island.

"How are you feeling?"

After setting her mug down, she lifted a shoulder then let it fall. "Conflicted." Her lips curved in a crooked grin. "On one hand, I'm ecstatically happy. Then when I remember what my 'friend' did, the murder and betrayal, I can't stop the sadness."

"It'll take time." I grasped her hand and threaded our fingers together.

"I know. And I'm lucky to have you."

I leaned over and tucked a piece of her dark hair behind her ear. "I'm the lucky one, Riley."

The sound of a motorboat carried on the breeze. Jaxon was here, which meant that it was time for me to leave for the meeting. We both got to our feet, and she wrapped her arms around me. I hugged her, inhaling the smell of hibiscus that clung to her hair.

She rose onto her toes and whispered, "Hurry back."

That went without saying. I would move mountains to be by her side.

———

IRRITATION BUZZED through me like an influx of coffee first thing in the morning. I'd arrived on the Pearl Harbor base at 0900, as requested by Daryl. It was important, and I wanted to talk with Ty and Mark, but leaving Riley behind made my skin crawl. The thought of something happening, of not being able to get to her in time, was too much to bear. It didn't matter that Ava was locked safely behind bars with no bail posted.

Everything was too fresh. The shark-tooth machete in Ava's duffel bag matched the marks on Charles's foot and would be compared to the injuries on the local barista and what was probably Mel's foot. Chances were good that it would match.

Jaxon offered to hang with her on the island until I was able to get back. That helped some, but I wanted to be the one spending time with her.

I had my answer—I wasn't reenlisting. It had been a torturous decision until Riley's life was at stake. When my contract was up, I was out.

I contacted Jack Davis with Gray Ghost Securities, and as soon as I was cleared of active duty, I would be on their payroll for missions. Our family had wealth, but we weren't used to being idle. Yet getting the surfboard business up and running and going out on rescue-and-recovery missions, we would have enough to stay busy.

"Hey." Ty leaned a hip against the counter in the break room. I was getting another coffee, something I shouldn't drink with so much aggravation seething below the surface.

"Meeting starts in two minutes. I tagged Mark. He'll be in here in a second." Ty's head notched up. "Correction—make that now."

I turned toward the door when Mark walked in. He wore a white button-down and black pants. As a government employee and an analyst, Mark didn't answer to the military regarding dress code or hair length.

"Have you found anything?" We'd agreed to elicit Mark's help but had kept it quiet, as there were too many unknowns. Somehow, the enemy was getting intel prior to our missions, and we were losing good men because of it. We needed to find the leak.

Mark ran his hand through his thick dark hair. "No. So far, everything is as usual. Ty said you pulled up some pictures."

We didn't have much time. I had them up as soon as I'd arrived and thought I found something. While blurry, the image was clear enough. Whoever it was had looked to the sky, maybe due to the Black Hawk's sound in the distance. The timing would've matched when we were airborne, flying overhead and sending imaging back. We crowded my desk, and I brought the picture back up. "Can you do anything to enhance this?" I pointed to the area we were scrutinizing.

"I should be able to," Mark answered.

It was difficult to tell, but the person didn't look like a member of the cartel. The Los Elegido members all had small skulls crossed with snakes tattooed on their faces. The person in the photo didn't have any visible ink. It was possible that a rebel group was involved, most likely from Venezuela.

Mark wasn't the only one we would enlist to help. Jaxon had placed a call to Liam, another contact with the Gray Ghost Security team. Through Liam's wife, they'd encountered and dealt with Colombian cartels and might have been able to fill in the missing pieces. With the clock ticking down to the next mission, we needed answers quickly.

Joe stuck his head in. "Meeting's starting."

We left Mark and headed into the conference room, where we took our seats at the long rectangular table. The meeting was about a new mission, not a recap of what had gone wrong a month before.

I glanced at the clock again, counting down the minutes until I could return to Riley.

Silence settled over us as the meeting began. Daryl was at the head of the table. We exchanged greetings. Then an image filled the large smart screen at the end of the room. Everyone's attention shifted to the building Daryl circled in San Antonio del Táchira, Venezuela.

"We've been monitoring the port where the Iranian ship docked. Not a lot of activity until last night. Several crates were unloaded and taken to another location. More came in to the dock, but our interest is on the ones that are left. As the deceased informant was a dead end, this is the next thing we'll be pursuing. We've established contact with a new informant, who provided proof of missiles and what could be nukes stacked together but have since been moved. Those weapons are out there. We leave in five days." Daryl turned to me with a shuttered expression. "A smaller contingent of men will carry out these orders. You'll remain on leave until they return."

Son of a bitch! Dread filled me, and for a few seconds, I couldn't move. With two weeks until my contract was up for renewal, he was benching me. I got it—Ty was still assigned to our unit through temporary addition orders, which would make it impossible for me to go on this one, as we were family. The last few missions had gone to hell. I didn't want my brother out there before we revealed the threat—possibly an internal one—

especially when several members of our team had died on the last three missions.

———

RILEY SAT between my legs in the sand, her back against my chest. The surf broke at our toes, and she rocked her heels, digging a little trench for them. Wispy clouds dotted the sky, and the sun chased away the slight chill from the recent rain.

I didn't want to go into details about the meeting, so the three of us had lunch then Jaxon took off, which was what I wanted—to be alone with Riley. "We need to talk about your apartment, about getting your stuff out."

She shuddered in my arms, and I nuzzled her neck. "I'm never going back there. Too many bad memories."

"Jaxon and I can pack it up for you. The lease is up in a week, isn't it?"

"Yes." She rested her head on me. "I haven't given any thought to where I want to go next."

"You would leave Hawaii?" I froze, waiting for her response. We'd told each other how we felt, but that wasn't a guarantee that she would stay after all she'd been through.

I was ready to plan our lives together and take the next step, but I wasn't sure what she was thinking. We hadn't known each other all that long. For me, it didn't matter. I could have met her three days ago, and my life would have been forever changed.

"No." She shifted in my arms, and I loosened them so she could turn and look at me. "I just found you. I'm not ready to let you go. I'll have to look for another place to stay."

I'd never lived with any of my past girlfriends, but Riley was different. Then another thought doused my hope, and my arms locked around her. "Are there too many bad memories here?"

I grasped her waist and lifted her to sit astride my lap so I could see the emotions playing over her face. The last thing I wanted to do was push her into something she wasn't ready for, even if I was.

A brilliant smile transformed her from beautiful to stunning. "That's not it at all. The encounter with Ava was horrifying and still upsets me. But we've created some amazing memories—and, well, you're here. I want to be with you because I love you."

My arms tightened around her, drawing her closer so I could kiss her senseless. "I love you too." Our lips met, and I teased hers open, deepening the kiss. Hunger for her buzzed in my head, making it difficult to pull back, but we had more to talk about before I took her to bed, which we wouldn't leave for a very long time. "I have a few more weeks until my contract is up for the Navy. I'm not re-upping."

"Okay." Confusion swirled in her pretty whiskey-colored eyes. "That's not a deal breaker for me. If you want to sign up for another term, I support you."

"It's time. I'm ready for something else." I tugged on her high ponytail. "I was hoping that you'd move here with me."

"Are you sure?" At my nod, she laughed, her face lit with a mesmerizing inner glow. "Then yes."

"That's not all." With the pad of my thumb, I caressed her plump lower lip. "I want to spend a lifetime with you. Will you marry me, Riley?"

"You're all I ever dreamed about, Xander. Yes, I'll marry you."

I took her mouth in a soul-searing kiss. While we kissed, I got to my feet, and her legs automatically wrapped around my waist as I carried her back to the cabin. The woman had changed my life. I would do everything to make her happy because, in my heart, it was clear that she was the one.

Despite the joy of having Riley here and with me, a bad feeling still lingered. No matter what, I couldn't shake the ominous sense that clung to me about my younger brother's imminent departure to Venezuela.

The End

Continue reading the Deadly Isles Special Ops series with
Bound by Secrets:
https://amymckinleyauthor.com/?page_id=693

Keep up with Amy's releases by joining her newsletter:
http://eepurl.com/dEBqJn

If you enjoyed reading TWISTED SECRETS as much as I did writing it, I hope you'll consider leaving a review.

ACKNOWLEDGMENTS

Each book comes with its own set of challenges. This entire series was written during 2020—which is enough to foretell the struggles from concept to creation. I'm fortunate to have the incredible team of authors and editors behind me, especially this year.

With heartfelt thanks to my amazing critique partners and fellow authors, Taylor Anhalt, Emily Albright, Kristin Kisska, and Candace Irving for providing insight, candor, and camaraderie from the first draft to the final edit.

To Kate B. and Taylor A., two incredible editors at Red Adept Editing, who did a fantastic job and made this story so much better. To T.E. Black for chatting at all hours and creating so many gorgeous covers for me.

Big thanks to Itsy Bitsy Book Bits Promotions for going above and beyond. To all the readers, bloggers, and reviewers who went out of their way to help and support this release— you're all so very generous and kind. Your support and encouragement continue to inspire me.

And last, but in no way least, to my husband, two daughters, and two sons, for supporting and believing in me while I follow my dreams. For their patience and understanding when the house is messy and general chaos reigns. I can't imagine life without them.

ABOUT THE AUTHOR

Amy McKinley is the *USA Today* Bestselling Author of the romantic suspense thriller Gray Ghost Novels, Deadly Isles Special Ops, Covert Recruits, Moonlit Destination Series, the Five Fates paranormal romance books, and several standalone titles. Her edge-of-your-seat books are filled with surprising twists and just the right amount of heat and danger. She lives in Illinois with her husband, two daughters, two sons, and three mischievous cats.

facebook.com/amymckinleyauthor
twitter.com/AmyMcKinley7
instagram.com/amymckinleyauthor
bookbub.com/authors/amy-mckinley

ALSO BY AMY MCKINLEY

Gray Ghost Novels

Moments That Define Us

Broken Circle

Eye of the Storm

Beneath the Surface

Vantage Point

Covert Threat

Marked for Death

Deadly Isles Special Ops

Hidden Secrets

Twisted Secrets

Bound by Secrets

Forged by Secrets

Covert Recruits (coming soon)

Irina

Sasha

Zena

Nadia

Katya

Standalone Titles

Shattered Melody

Siren's Call: Cursed Seas

Fake Fiancé (A Second Chance Office Romance)

Moonlit Destination Series

Moonlit Whisper

Moonlit Kiss

Moonlit Mirage

Five Fates Series

Hidden

Taken

www.ingramcontent.com/pod-product-compliance
Lightning Source LLC
Chambersburg PA
CBHW070942190726
48292CB00004B/1302